CIRCLE OF AIR

THE WITCH'S PROGRESS
BOOK ONE

LEAH R CUTTER

KNOTTED ROAD PRESS

Circle of Air
Witch's Heart: Book 1
Copyright © 2018 Leah Cutter
All rights reserved
Published by Knotted Road Press
www.KnottedRoadPress.com

ISBN: 978-1-644-70-101-0

Cover by Miblart.com

Interior design copyright © 2018 Knotted Road Press http://www.
KnottedRoadPress.com

Reviews
It's true. Reviews help me sell more books. If you've enjoyed this story, please consider leaving a review of it on your favorite site.

Come someplace new…
Are you a traveler? Do you enjoy exploring strange new worlds, new cultures, new people?

Journey into the various lands envisioned by Leah R Cutter.

Sign up for my newsletter and I'll start you on your travels with a free copy of my book, *The Island Sampler*.

http://www.LeahCutter.com/newsletter/

Buy More!
Did you know that you can buy directly from the Knotted Road Press website?

https://www.knottedroadpress.com/shop/

ALSO BY LEAH R CUTTER

Urban/Contemporary Fantasy Series

The Shadow Wars Trilogy

The Raven and the Dancing Tiger

The Guardian Hound

War Among the Crocodiles

The Cassie Stories

Poisoned Pearls

Tainted Waters

Spoiled Harvest

Bloodied Ice

The Witch's Progress

Circle of Air

Circle of Fire

Circle of Water

Circle of Earth

Seattle Trolls

The Changeling Troll

The Princess Troll

The Fairy-Bridge Troll

The Troll-Demon War

The Troll-Human War

The Troll-Troll War

The Clockwork Fairy Kingdom

The Clockwork Fairy Kingdom

The Maker, the Teacher, and the Monster

The Dwarven Wars

The Chronicles of Franklin

Franklin Versus The Popcorn Thief

Franklin Versus The Soul Thief

Franklin Versus The Child Thief

Epic Fantasy Series

The Fallen Elves

Ruins of the Gods

Stairs of the Gods

Cities of the Gods

Graves of the Gods

Houses of the Dead

Houses Divided

Houses Fallen

Houses Reborn

Forgotten Gods

A Wind Blown Torment

A Stone Strewn Clash

A Sea Washed Victory

The Tanesh Empire Trilogy

The Glass Magician

The Desert Heart

The Ghost Dog

Science Fiction

The Long Run

Project Nemesis

Project Nyx

Project Tisiphone

Project Persephone

War of the Allied Worlds

The Labors of Darius Linard

Huli Intergalactic: Science/Space Fantasy

Origins

The Strawberry Girl

Mysteries

The Purloined Letter Opener

The Tell Tale Heart Pin

Dancer in Darkness

Trophy Hunters

The Alvin Goodfellow Case Files

The Rabbit Mysteries

The Shredded Veil Mysteries

Mystery, Crime, and Mayhem

THE CIRCLES OF WITCHCRAFT

ix

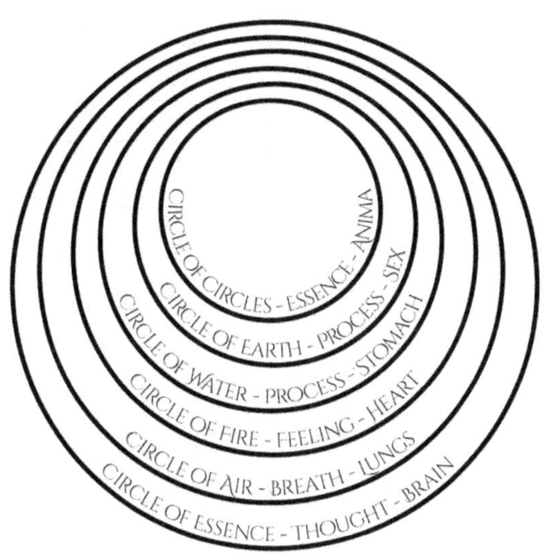

CHAPTER 1

The smell of rotten wood and wet plaster permeates the streets of Portland now that the flood waters have receded. Mold, too, covers every surface that had been underwater, black inky lines that look like a child gone mad with charcoal. More bloated bodies have been discovered in the first floor rooms of some of the buildings. The cost of lives, livestock, and goods is astronomical. Though I objected to being brought in to build the next bridge so early, my superiors at the Pacific Bridge Company were correct: I needed to see this damage so I fully understood what the consequences of failure might bring.

Wilson Evermore, Civil Engineer, 1894

Tara watched, delighted, as the bright green hummingbird flitted around the feeder she'd set up earlier that week. The blue glass feeder swayed slightly on the metal stand jutting up from the cold iron handrail of the balcony. The hummingbird—one of the local Annas—rested after circling a few more times, dipping his head into the bright red-glass flower and sipping the nectar contained inside.

She hadn't been certain that she'd get any birds. The apartment she rented was close to the train station in downtown Portland, not in one of the neighborhoods that was full of greenery and parks. While the waterfront below her held a lot of blackberry bramble, there weren't a lot of trees.

Underneath the feeder, pressed up against the low balcony wall, stood a long bench covered in potted plants: rosemary, English lavender, spearmint, variegated marjoram, basil (three varieties), curly-leaf parsley, purple sage, borage, French sorrel, to name just a few. Tara kept the plants well-trimmed or they would have spilled over the sides of the bench.

She needed the herbs not just for her salads and teas but for her magical potions as well, so none of the leaves she clipped ever went to waste.

The balcony of her shared apartment faced northeast. Below, she could see the Willamette River. It was the main reason she'd agreed to rent this place, so that she could be on the river. (Well, both the view and the big balcony.) Tara had always tried to live close to the water ever since she'd moved to Portland fourteen years before, when she'd just gotten out of college and foolishly followed her college sweetheart across country, moving from Wisconsin to Oregon.

If Tara could afford it, she'd buy herself a house on a river bank. But she already had to work two jobs in order to pay her share of the rent of the two bedroom apartment. And she expected the rent to go up again in about a month's time, when their current contract finished.

That Friday, Tara had the afternoon shift at the shop, so she got to sit on the balcony and enjoy the peaceful morning air while sipping her tea. Today, she'd used a beautiful black Assam for the base, to which she'd added cocoa nibs, some dried apple bits, a splash of vanilla, and two freshly picked spearmint leaves. It was one of the smoother teas she'd created, and a regular favorite.

It wasn't that quiet, as usual—too much city traffic seeped up from the busy streets behind her, the constant hum of cars across the Steel Bridge almost soothing. As summer had yet to take a solid hold, the air was chilly, and Tara wore a soft, gray cotton work shirt over her T-shirt and jeans.

Tara didn't wear any makeup—she considered herself pretty enough with wide-spaced blue eyes, soft brown hair that fell to just below her shoulder blades, and clear white skin that would freckle in the summer sun. Yes, she carried more weight than what was considered popular these days, primarily around her middle, but being almost six feet tall, she carried it well. Plus, a lot of that weight was actually muscle from swimming and yoga.

"Ewww. What's that thing?" said Sharon, stepping out onto the balcony and chasing away the tiny bird. "It's not going to shit all over everything, is it?"

"No, it won't," Tara said with a sigh. She picked up her tea mug from the wrought iron table beside her. Damn it. Empty already.

At least that gave her an excuse to leave and get out of Sharon's way, despite the fact that Tara loved spending her mornings out here and would sit out here on the hard iron chairs all day, watching the river and the traffic going up and down it.

The hummingbird buzzed by the feeder. He made a loud thrumming noise as he passed.

"Get away!" Sharon said, shaking her hands frantically in front of her face.

"He isn't about to attack you," Tara said mildly.

"How do you know?" Sharon said, glaring over at Tara. "Those things are vicious."

"It's more scared of you than you are of it," Tara said, not wanting to point out that the tiny bird wouldn't even take up a third of Sharon's meaty palm.

"You don't know how scared I can get," Sharon said stubbornly.

Tara just shrugged. That was true, actually. Tara didn't know how frightened Sharon could get, though Tara suspected that if she tried, she could whip up a concoction or a brew for Sharon that would cause Sharon to be utterly terrified.

Just for a moment, Tara let herself imagine what that might look like. Sharon had blonde hair straight out of a bottle that she wore poofed up around her face, a modern take on a 1950s bouffant. Her gray-green eyes looked tired that morning, and the makeup on her pale white skin did a poor job of hiding the dark circles-- staying up too late reading or watching TV, probably. Sharon wore her typical work outfit, a nice, lightweight black jacket over a short-sleeved white blouse and black slacks—office wear for the wannabe manager. Sharon worked as a technical writer and really didn't need to dress so formally, however, she had her sights set on her boss' job.

Could Tara rig up a potion that would make Sharon's hair stand on end? Like one of those cartoon figures who'd just touched an electric wire? The fear would make Sharon's face grow ashen and no amount of makeup would bring color to her cheeks. How huge would her eyes get, if she was truly frightened? How wide would her mouth stretch with screams?

Tara shook her head, banishing the image. She wasn't like that. Wasn't that type of witch, though she'd originally trained under exactly that sort of witch when she'd first discovered her powers here in Portland.

The hummingbird buzzed the small balcony again.

"You see!" Sharon said. "Mean, nasty thing. It's going to keep me from enjoying the balcony this summer."

"No, it won't," Tara said, though now she wasn't sure. Maybe the hummingbird had the good taste to dislike Sharon and would try to chase her away.

"Fine," Sharon said. "But you're the one who will have to clean all the bird shit off the chairs."

Tara nodded rather than say something, as she wasn't certain she could stay polite.

Sharon stomped off, slamming the sliding glass door leading to the living room of the apartment behind her.

The hummingbird very politely flitted by the feeder again, landing delicately on the stand, cocking his head from one side to the other while looking at Tara, making a *click-click-click* sound.

Huh. Maybe he really didn't like Sharon as he was no longer divebombing the balcony.

"I don't care much for her either," Tara told the bird softly. "But she has the largest bedroom, with her own bathroom, and so pays the majority of the rent. I can't live here without her."

The hummingbird clicked at her again before going to feed, as if he was an old aunt, *tsking* at her bad fortune.

It might not be Tara's problem for too much longer, if the rent really did get raised an astronomical amount next month.

She'd just have to find another place to live, close enough to see the water. But with housing prices rising so fast, leaping higher than her wages, that might become a big problem.

The buzzing of her phone brought her out of her morning meditation. It was Patricia.

One of the advantages to living so close to downtown was that Tara didn't own a car and could walk to work.

The disadvantage was that anytime something went wrong, Patricia, the owner, tended to call Tara first.

"Tara, darling, I'm so sorry to bother you! I hope I'm not waking you," came Patricia's breezy tone.

"Am awake. Mostly," Tara said truthfully. It would be another hour or so before she was fully "there". Tara enjoyed what she called a slow roll in the mornings rather than jolting herself up and having to run at full speed.

"You know that normally I wouldn't ask, but Han Su just called and asked if she could have part of the morning off," Patricia said. "Something about registration and paperwork."

Tara sighed. While she adored the sly humor of her co-worker, Han Su tended to not understand deadlines. Those were for other people, not free spirits like her.

"I can come in early," Tara said slowly. "But—"

"Thank you! Thank you!" Patricia said. "I knew you'd come to the rescue. I'd work the shift myself but I already have so many things scheduled!"

"Patricia!" Tara said loudly before her boss could hang up.

"Yes?" Patricia asked with just a hint of impatience in her voice, as if Tara was the one calling for a favor now.

"That will put my hours into overtime for the week," Tara said.

A quiet sigh came across the line. "You could just not work next week…"

"We've tried that before and it's never worked out like that," Tara reminded her.

"Fine, I'll authorize the overtime," Patricia said.

Tara could tell that Patricia really wanted to say

something more, or even warn Tara to not let it happen again. However, it wasn't Tara's fault that she'd ended up working so many hours this week. Between Han Su and inventory, there wasn't much else that Tara could do.

Plus, she needed the money.

"See you later," Tara said breezily, cutting the connection before she could hear Patricia complain.

It wasn't as if Patricia couldn't afford it. She wasn't dependent on the shop's income. Patricia was independently wealthy and lived in one of the mansions in south Portland with her two long-haired ragdoll cats.

The hummingbird came back to the feeder again, choosing a different red flower to sip from before flitting off to do its business.

Tara rose to her feet and stretched her arms over her head before leaning over and brushing her fingers against the cool concrete floor. The backs of her legs were still a little sore from the yoga class she'd taken the day before.

She didn't like to think how much more effort it took to stay in shape now that she was thirty-eight. Maybe she'd have to take up bike riding or something.

She shuddered at the image. Of course, she'd tried it, more than once. She lived in Portland, after all. But it had never suited her, not even as a kid.

Swimming though—she could stay in the water all day long. She'd actually planned on heading down to the Y and taking a swim later that morning. Then maybe spending some time studying, memorizing the Latin names of plants, as well as their traditional medicinal, culinary, utilitarian, and magical properties.

Tara was a witch of the first circle, the circle of thought. She had a lot to learn before she could pass within, to the next circle, the circle of breath, also sometimes called the circle of air.

However, all her plans had just flown away, as quickly as the hummingbird who had just taken off. Now she had to call her coworker Han Su, find out when she needed to leave, then probably pack both a lunch as well as a dinner.

Maybe the store would be quiet and she could spend more time studying…

But Tara doubted that her luck would be that good. Particularly on a Friday afternoon at the start of the summer. Tourist season was just getting started. The store would be incredibly busy from now until October.

Tara nodded to the hummingbird who'd returned for just one more sip before heading inside to start her day.

"YE OLDE MAGICK SHOPPE" WAS A POPULAR TOURIST destination in the heart of the Pearl District in downtown Portland. It was a storefront that had been built into a converted warehouse, so the walls were new but the floor was the original scratched up and scarred wood. The ceilings were eighteen feet high, giving the room an airy feeling. Though no direct sunlight could shine into the tall front windows, they still let in an incredible amount of ambient light, even during the rainy winter months.

The front of the shop wasn't that big, about twenty by sixteen, with the counter smack in the center of the room. Shelves lined the walls and contained a variety of "magical" items, such as sparkly wands for kids, "blessed" candles in every color and scent, books about the ghosts and haunted places in Portland, crystals and geodes, wooden pyramids, and copper-lined bracelets.

Many wannabe witches dropped by, exclaiming that the shop had a good feel to it, a presence—frequently stating that they'd been drawn there. They would tell Tara stories about the charms they were creating, the spells they'd cast, even the sightings they'd had of ghosts, UFOs, and various other things.

While Tara tried to be sympathetic, her co-worker Han Su was shameless. She'd speak to tourists in a heavy Asian accent with broken syntax, then hand sell one of the most expensive geodes or crystal balls to the customer, going on and on about her Chinese ancestors.

Never mind that Han Su was actually Vietnamese, second generation, raised in Portland, and spoke perfectly good English.

The tourists paid good money for trinkets then were on their way, a constant stream of knickknacks flowing out and money flowing in.

However, the front of the store was literally just that, a front, for the actual magic shop in the back.

In the far right corner of the back wall stood an open door to the second room. Patricia called it "hiding in plain sight." Most of the tourists who came in never even poked their head in the room.

Those who found the room had power, whether they knew it or not.

The back of the shop resembled a modern apothecary, or maybe even an expensive tea shop. Dark wooden shelves stuck out from the bright white walls. Precisely placed cream-colored porcelain containers lined the shelves—the kind generally used to hold coffee beans. Handwritten signs listed the various dried herbs, roots, and spices.

A long counter ran the length of the room, in front of the shelves, at the perfect height for Tara to work at (while Han Su complained about it being too high all the time, as she was just over five feet tall). An old-fashioned balance scale dominated a corner of the counter, used for precisely measuring out quantities of dried herbs. It had a large scoop on one side of the balance and a flat metal disc on the other. Underneath the scale, a pyramid-shaped case held all the various weights.

Two large stainless steel refrigerators hummed against the wall to the right, containing all the fresh herbs.

And today, Tara's lunch, as well as her dinner.

Tara carefully slid the large stalks of basil and lemongrass to the side as she placed her lunch and dinner on the top shelf. Han Su was still standing behind her, thanking her profusely for taking the remainder of her shift.

"I don't know what I was thinking!" Han Su said

again. "I really thought the deadline for signing up for summer classes was next week, not this week."

"It's okay," Tara said. She shrugged and gave the other woman a conspiratorial grin. "I need the overtime."

"Ooooh, you got overtime this week?" Han Su said.

Though Han Su was twenty-four, it was easy for Tara to see the old Asian grandmother that Han Su would eventually turn into. Han Su kept her long hair primly tied back into a neat bun at the back of her head. She wore an old-fashioned apron while she worked in the store, one made out of beige duck cloth, meant to help convey the image that she wasn't fully American. Under that, she had on a modest soft orange short-sleeved shirt and gray slacks.

"I earned that overtime," Tara gently reminded Han Su.

"I suppose," Han Su said, nodding. "You work too much."

Tara snorted. "I don't live with my family," she pointed out. She had to work more than just at the shop in order to pay her rent.

"It's tradition!" Han Su protested.

Tara opened her mouth then shut it again. She'd met Han Su's parents. They'd both been born in America and were effortlessly chic. Probably the only reason why they'd agree for their bohemian daughter to continue living at home while trying to complete her fifth (sixth?) attempt at a college degree was so that they would continue to have the opportunity to tame her.

Good luck with that.

"Why are you taking summer classes anyway?" Tara asked as they moved to the front of the store. Only three customers browsed the shelves at that point, but Tara was expecting a complete rush in about an hour, right around noon, when one of the local Portland tour buses disgorged their passengers half a block away.

Despite her high society leanings, Patricia was a sharp shopkeeper. She stayed on top of the inventory and always seemed to understand the trends before they began, stocking the latest gimmick just before it was discovered by the masses. (She'd stocked a whole collection of notebooks with birds on them one week before the show about "put a bird on it" aired.) Plus, she'd chosen the perfect location for the store in terms of walk-by customers.

"Don't tell anyone," Han Su said, staying on the customer side of the counter and leaning over while Tara took her place behind it, "but there's a new playwriting class that I'm taking."

Tara tried not to roll her eyes. Han Su really wanted to be a writer (as did Sharon, her flatmate). They frequently got into long debates about the virtues of outlining versus writing into the dark, what various markets were hot at the time and writing for them, as well as sharing tidbits about their very different writing styles.

However, Han Su tended to take class after class instead of actually sitting down and writing. Sharon wrote more, or at least pretended to, as she was on her social media feeds most of the time when she was supposed to be writing.

Tara had no desire whatsoever to be a writer. Writing up descriptions of the stock always fell to Han Su or Patricia, as Tara tended to just look at the thing and then baldly describe it. ("It's a candle and it smells pretty.") It was Han Su who came up with the various notes around the store describing the merchandise, talking about the primeval power of the pyramids, the healing abilities of the cooper lined bracelets, the mystical enchantments of the crystals.

"Go sign up for your classes," Tara said, shooing Han Su out of the shop as a customer approached the counter.

"I'll see you at the party tonight, right?" Han Su said as she untied the back of her apron.

Tara nearly groaned. She'd forgotten that the "party" —basically, a meeting of the coven—was tonight. "I can make an appearance," Tara said. "I won't be able to stay late."

Han Su pouted. "You never stay late. You work too much."

Tara merely raised a single eyebrow at Han Su, silently pointing out that Tara wasn't even supposed to be working at this time.

"Okay! Bye! See you later!" Han Su said brightly, waving as she left.

"How can I help you?" Tara said, smiling as she turned to the customer waiting patiently.

The rest of the afternoon passed quickly, a steady stream of customers and questions, with barely enough time for her to sneak in drinks of the homemade smoothie she'd brought for lunch. Fortunately, it was really tasty, so she kept going back for more. Today, it had fresh golden raspberries, spinach, kale, bok choy, cucumber and celery for the veggies part, along with homemade coconut milk yogurt as well as coconut milk, vanilla, and protein powder.

Right around six o'clock came the usual dinner lull, and Tara was able to dig into the mason jar salad she'd brought. She'd cut up just a few leaves of the variegated marjoram and mixed those in, along with some basil, borage, and French sorrel. They gave a nice tang to the various lettuces and cabbage. Plus bacon, of course, and hard boiled eggs.

After the dinner lull many of the local witches stopped by for supplies for the weekend and for the solstice next week. Tara spent at least half her time in the back, measuring out ingredients and bagging them for her customers. A dozen internet orders came in as well that Tara was able to box up, ready to drop off at the post office in the morning. Kyle came by early in the evening, then promised to return later to give Tara a lift to the coven meeting.

Just as Tara was getting ready to close up shop, an older gentleman showed up. Tara was surprised—she hadn't heard the bell ring when the front door opened. She just looked up, and there he was, in the backroom with her.

She tried to get a good look at him, however, it seemed as though he stood in shadows which made his expression and features indistinct. She had the impression that he was shorter and rounder than she was, but not soft, no, he gave off a feeling of granite. She assumed he was white, as his face did appear fairly pale. He wore not only a fancy brown wool suit coat, but a vest and pants as well. His white shirt was the brightest thing about him, held tightly together at the collar with a string tie. He doffed his bowler-like hat to her as he stepped closer to the counter.

"Can I help you?" Tara asked, blinking and trying to see his face. It wavered as if it was underwater. Then again, he also smelled of the sea, of kelp and salt.

"Maybe," the man said, cocking his head to the side. "Tell me, do you have any dried purple heather? *Calluna vulgaris?*"

"We do," Tara said. She reached for the jar on the shelf behind her.

Opening the jar filled the room with the scent of a warm summer hillside.

"Tell me, what are the properties of heather?" the man asked.

Tara suddenly felt as though she stood in front of her first teacher, Miss Lucy.

"Protection, luck, and peace," Tara replied. "Carry it in a sachet to protect against violence. Hang it from the ceiling in the northeast corner of the house to promote peace. Tie it together with dried clover for luck."

"It also brings rain," the man reminded her.

"Yes, yes of course," Tara said. "Burn it with sword ferns to cause it to rain."

"And what are the real properties?" the man asked.

"I…I don't understand," Tara said purposefully. As part of her lore learning, she'd had to memorize both parts of every herb, the traditional, old-fashioned magick as well as the true magical properties. Sometimes they overlapped, often they didn't.

However, Tara didn't want to start listing off the hidden, secret parts of her learning. She didn't know this man. She was certain he was human, as the hairs on the back of her neck didn't stand and warn her of some sort of *other*.

Yet, there was something off with him, and she didn't know him.

"Heather is used by the head, to clear the thoughts of the practitioners before a the start of a prayer circle," the man admonished her.

"Yes," Tara said slowly. "And by the lungs, to promote deeper breathing," she added, wanting to show that she wasn't completely stupid.

"Exactly!" the man said with a nod. "Six paths to the light," he said. "Six circles to pass through. Head, lungs, heart, stomach, and sex, until finally, anima."

Tara nodded. He used the older terms for the tenants of witchcraft, but he knew the true path, where the real magic lay.

However, instead of making her more comfortable with this man, possibly acknowledging that he was a witch like her, it just made her more wary.

She didn't trust this creature, and more and more he was starting to change from man into other, though physically he retained his human-like form.

If only she could see his face clearly!

Silence held the pair of them taut, staring at each other.

What did he want? He seemed to be searching for her soul.

Tara tried to look away but she couldn't.

Cold air whipped around Tara, blowing like a storm across an ice-laden river. The man in front of her grew darker. The strong smell of wet sisal rope filled the space.

Tara jumped when the bell over the door of the shop rang, the weird binding holding her still breaking.

"Excuse me," she said, slipping out from behind the counter and practically racing into the other room.

It wasn't another customer, but merely Kyle, who had returned for he like he'd said he would.

"I'll be just a minute," Tara assured him, though a part of her wanted to go and throw her arms around him.

He wouldn't have taken that well, however. Kyle was uncomfortable with any physical contact, even handshakes.

Tara turned back to room full of herbs, bracing herself before stepping back inside.

The room was empty. The container for the heather was back on the shelf.

Tara quickly turned around. No one besides Kyle stood in the shop. How had the man slipped out?

"Did you see anyone else here in the shop?" Tara asked.

"Not a soul," Kyle said seriously. He was usually serious. Only a few people, and Tara felt herself lucky enough to be included in that group, knew that Kyle could be a goofball as well, his white teeth practically shining in his black face. He kept his head shaved smooth, and oiled, which gave him a regal appearance. He was taller than she was, a six foot three wall of walking muscle. Over his plain T-shirt and jeans he frequently wore a funky vest. Tonight, it was a red-and-white bold print that had its roots in Afrofuturism.

Kyle had a timeless quality to him. He could have been as young as twenty or as old as fifty. Tara had only recently learned that he was actually forty-four.

"There was a man in here, when you came into the shop," Tara said as she stepped into the back room. She still smelled the river in here, could still feel the wet ropes and hear the cawing of seagulls.

"There's no one here," Kyle pointed out. "And no one came by me."

"And the jar he'd asked about is back on the shelf," Tara mused. She went and opened the heather, the fresh scent banishing her impressions of the river.

Though instead of just bringing the scent of sunshine, an undercurrent of rain was mingled with it.

Tara shook her head, but the scent of rain remained.

While Tara might be many things, overly imaginative wasn't one of them. She closed up the jar and thought for a moment before looking back to Kyle.

"I don't know if he was here or not," Tara admitted. "But something just happened."

"Maybe you fell asleep and dreamed about him," Kyle said. "Do I need to be jealous of your dream man?"

Tara snorted. "More like a nightmare man," she assured Kyle. "No need for jealousy." It wasn't that the pair of them were a couple—far from it, as Kyle preferred men. However, Kyle had stood in as Tara's beard at least on a couple of occasions, and their pretend dates had always gone well.

"I will protect you," Kyle said gallantly, taking a heroic stance, as if he wore a cape or something.

Tara rolled her eyes. "Goof," she said. "Come on. Or we'll be late."

Still, she checked the stockroom before she left as well, making sure that they were truly alone, before she closed the shop and locked the door.

Whoever that man was, whatever he was, she hoped she'd seen the last of him.

She feared, though, that this was just their first encounter.

CHAPTER 2

The task ahead of me is quite daunting. The combined waters of the Willamette and the Columbia rivers, swollen with runoff from the mountains, regularly flood the region. The old timers recollect floods coming through every three to five years. Yet my superiors want me to ensure that the next generation of bridges will never be washed away. I've developed stronger footings, as well as designs that lift the spans high into the heavens. Still, I fear this won't be enough. The true task is to prevent the floods from striking the bridges in the first place. To that effect, I've applied for funding for an expedition to travel further upstream, to see if it's possible to deal with the problem long before it reaches the fair city of Portland.

Wilson Evermore, Civil Engineer, 1896

THE COVEN WAS MEETING AT GILMORE'S HOUSE, UP IN Arlington Heights. It was an old craftsman house that was in beautiful shape but hadn't been "modernized," so it still had a separate formal living room, dining room, and kitchen (instead of the open floor plan that was so popular and the ruin of many a good space, at least in Tara's opinion.)

Parking was a bitch, as always, but Kyle managed to squeeze his Mini-Cooper in front of a van. It always amazed Tara how Kyle was able to fold himself into his car, but the cooper had a surprising amount of headroom, particularly for people as tall as them.

The night was softer out here. Crickets and cicadas sang above the sound of traffic. Tara was glad for her work shirt, as the temperature had dropped with the setting of the sun. She walked to the house next to Kyle, neither of them saying anything, as was their habit. Kyle was one of the few individuals that Tara could share that kind of silent communing with each other, enjoying each other's company without saying a word.

Gilmore's house saw on three quarters an acre, practically unheard of in the city. The backyard was built on a gentle slope, with three tiers. The top layer held an artificial mound that hid a modern pump for the water that encircled the area.

Tara knew it wasn't an enchantment—it was practically impossible to create magical artifacts, despite what all the myths proclaimed—but it always seemed to her that all the sounds of the outside world, the traffic and the planes, stopped as soon as she stepped into the backyard. All she could hear was the tinkling of the water.

The first tier up from the house contained a small meditation maze. It was made out of found stones. Instead of being circular, the maze was oval in order to fit the space. The stones led the walker along a winding path inward toward a small circular bowl in the center. Six circles made up the maze, one for each circle of power.

Tara had been allowed to walk the maze for the first time two years ago, during summer solstice. While walking, she'd had to focus her own thoughts and banish the illusions that the coven set for her, to stay true to the path before her, and arrive at the center gazing pond without misstep.

It had been her final test, a test of practicum, as it were. Tara hadn't at first known if she'd passed when she reached the inner circle unscathed. The gazing pond had held nothing but dark water for her. Usually, it showed images, either the past or the future, to the initiate when they finished walking the maze.

However, the pond wasn't the final arbiter of Tara's passing the test. Sheila had declared that Tara was now to be recognized as a full initiate of the first circle, the circle of thought (or brain, as the man had called it).

Since then, Tara had been studying for the next circle, the circle of breath (or lungs.) The other circles that lay before her were feeling, (heart), then process (stomach), roots (sex), and finally, if she lived long enough, anima, or the animating force that surrounded everything else.

Very few practitioners reached the sixth circle. It was why most covens were made up of six or eleven witches, or even sixteen: one or more of each of the outer circles, with a single anima practitioner.

Tara had taken over five years to move from merely practicing to the full first circle, while most who came to their power later in life only took a year or so. In part, that was because Tara had switched covens. Miss Lucy, for all her power, wasn't focused on bringing light to the world, just drawing more power to herself and those she protected, no matter the cost.

Miss Lucy's teachings had never sat well with Tara. She blamed her long association with that coven on her inexperience, not knowing there was another way. However, in her heart of hearts, Tara had known all along that she'd fallen in with a bad crowd, and then had done nothing to extricate herself.

Come winter solstice, Tara figured she'd be able to move from the circle of thought to the circle of air. It involved a lot of study on her part, to learn the herbs, oils, and concoctions traditionally associated with the new level, as well as building the strength to put those ingredients to use and perform real magic.

"You okay?" Kyle asked after a bit, while Tara still stood at the bottom of Gilmore's backyard.

"Yeah," Tara said. She shook her head and took a deep breath, allowing the peace of the garden to seep into her soul.

She didn't like that she still smelled rain in the air, though no rain was predicted for days, possibly weeks.

"You need to banish that man of your nightmares," Kyle said sternly.

Tara glanced at him, smiling to herself at the stern picture the tall black man presented. He was almost intimidating. Or maybe he would be to anyone who hadn't spent a night the previous week watching bad 1970s teen-dramas and laughing themselves silly.

"That guy is already gone," Tara said, lying. Then she paused and asked, "Should I mention him to Sheila? I'm not sure I want to bother the head of the coven."

Kyle thought about Tara's question for a moment before he shook his head. "Only if he returns," he said.

"Deal," Tara said, nodding. She didn't want to bother Sheila with just a bad dream, though Tara didn't usually have bad dreams, or any dreams at all.

Together, Tara and Kyle climbed the hill to the second tier, where most of the others in the coven were waiting. The area was flat and grassy. Sometimes they had a small fire in the center, that the witches could dance around as they brought in the new year on the solstice.

Almost everyone else was there already. Only Bernie was missing, and he was constantly late. Tara would think that a practitioner of process would understand how to be on time.

The coven only had three males out of eleven, Kyle, Bernie and Gilmore. Traditionally, witches were female, not male. However, Portland was a progressive town and made allowances. Thinking about it, it was one of the things that had surprised Tara, that her old-fashioned visitor was male.

Had he been a witch? Or something else? Tara was aware that there were other beings—spirits, ghosts, as well as the true *other*. However, as she was still only of the first circle, she didn't know anything about them.

Tara shook her head, banishing all thought of him.

He'd just been in her imagination, despite the fact that Tara was at her heart more practical than anything else.

"WE COME TOGETHER TO CELEBRATE THE GODDESS Brigid, defender of the earth, the god Samil, warrior for the people, along with the fullness of the season and the blessings of the moon," Sheila intoned, bringing the attention of everyone to her.

Sheila was the head of the coven, their anima practitioner, a short Mexican woman. While Sheila had the appearance of someone half her age, she was actually in her sixties. She carefully bleached her hair, hiding the gray by lightening it from its natural black to a ginger color. She hid the faded brown of her eyes with dark-colored contacts. Her face was remarkably free of wrinkles, which Tara believed to be natural, though possibly Sheila had had some work done. Her hands were what gave away her true age, the blue veins displayed across the back, the fingers boney, with age spots still showing.

She stood in the center of the circle, wearing a long flowing dress made out of a bright green cotton, with colorful yellow and red flowers embroidered across the yoke and around the hem. The short sleeves revealed powerful, muscular arms. She kept her ginger hair tied back in a tight bun that sat high on the back of her head.

Tara stood with Kyle on the one side and Han Su on the other. Both were more advanced than she was. Han Su had recently moved to the circle of feelings, while Kyle was still in the circle of process.

Tara wondered if Kyle would stay in the circle of process and never move beyond, to the root, or, as the gentleman that evening had reminded her, sex. One of the reasons for Kyle's aversion to touch was because he'd been gang-raped as a young man. Though it had been over two decades before, Kyle still bore the psychic wounds. Tara knew that her friendship with the tall black man had helped him recover, particularly having someone who accepted him as he was and never asked for more.

Han Su had started with the coven after Tara, then had advanced more quickly than Tara. Not because Han Su was a more powerful witch than Tara, but primarily because she hadn't had to unlearn the teachings that Tara had had to.

Shelia had originally been hesitant to take Tara on because of her initial training. Patricia had finally intervened for her, calling in some unknown favor between the two covens.

It was one of the reasons why Tara kept working for Patricia, despite how the other woman treated her sometimes.

Tara participated in the litany with the others, calling on the moon to bless them, sending out prayers and healing into the world. They didn't perform any magic that night: tonight was their usual midmonth gathering. They'd meet again on the solstice in five days' time, to celebrate the length of the light, the shortest night, and to draw from their powers in order to perform a deep healing.

The world needed it right now. Tara felt helpless sometimes, despite how she worked with the others to heal the deadly wounds being inflicted on their society at the present.

Tara briefly held hands with the others at the end of their ritual. It was one of the reasons why Kyle always stood beside her: it wasn't that he tolerated her touch better, but that she understood and would lock only pinkies with him, not insisting that they fully clasp hands palm to palm.

As the circle broke, Tara felt lighter, as usual. The air seemed more clear and crisp, though that might have also been the falling temperature.

Kyle had moved over to talk with Bernie about something, though he'd promised Tara a ride home soon. The rest of the coven would meet and talk far into the night, possibly even practice some magic, prepare a potion or two, everyone gathered together in the large kitchen, laughing and talking. Tara had to work most of the next day—an early shift at the store, then babysitting that evening—so she couldn't stay up late. Not if she expected to be able to function tomorrow.

Aaloka, Sheila's second in command and a long time fifth circle practitioner, came up to talk with Tara as the group was breaking up. Aaloka had no desire to ever move on to the final circle, which made her a perfect companion for Sheila.

"Blessed be," Aaloka said as she put her palms together in front of her chest and bowed her head low to Tara.

"Blessed be," Tara responded, echoing Aaloka's movements. Though witches didn't normally greet each other that way, Aaloka's family came from New Delhi. She only wore a sari on nights of performance and celebration. Tonight she wore a casual blue-denim shirt tucked into a pair of skinny black jeans.

Tara always felt like an Amazon standing next to Aaloka. The woman was tiny, barely reaching Tara's chest, and bird thin. While Sheila was short, she felt solid to Tara, a tough mountain that would never blow over. Aaloka was more like a willow—not about to be uprooted or broken, however, Tara always had to wonder if Aaloka would sway in a strong enough wind.

"How do your studies go?" Aaloka asked as she usually did. She was the one who administered the oral part of the test for the circles.

"Well," Tara said. She wasn't really lying. She'd put in the hours studying and memorizing lists of herbs. She needed to add more practice to her curriculum, though. It was difficult, particularly given her flatmate.

And whenever Tara did make a mistake, the results were more disastrous as she learned to call winds and make them dance around her. Just learning thoughts and control had been a more internal art. Air was external. The circles were purposefully structured that way, an internal art followed by an external, then back to internal, and so on.

"How is your garden growing?" Aaloka asked.

Tara blinked in surprise. Generally, Aaloka inquired more about where Tara was in terms of her studies. Asking about her garden was completely new.

"Really well," Tara said. "The spearmint would like to take over the entire bench, of course. However, the sage has heard the spearmint's bid and would like to raise it. The thyme, too, might be a contender before the end of the summer. And I'm not even going to talk about the oregano."

Aaloka grinned. "That's always the way. First one thing decides to take over the world, then the next. You are staying on top of them though, yes?"

Tara wasn't really sure what Aaloka was asking. "I make the plants behave, keep their runners to themselves."

"Good," Aaloka said, though from her tone, it was obvious that Tara was missing the point.

"Oh!" Tara said, not sure why it was important but deciding that maybe it was. "And I had a hummingbird —an Anna—at the feeder this morning."

"That's wonderful news," Aaloka said, nodding and smiling as if Tara had actually gotten the quiz right. "The hummingbird is a representation of the great Hayvu, the goddess of the western winds. You must be making great progress to draw one of her birds to you."

"Or it could be the feeder," Tara pointed out. That was one of the problems she had with Aaloka. Everything wasn't necessarily the fault of a god or goddess. Sometimes the responsibility lay in the actions of people, usually when they didn't listen to their hearts.

Aaloka cocked her head to one side and looked quizzically at Tara. "Because you live in such a green area and there are always so many birds to contend with, right? Besides the pigeons at the train station."

Tara opened her mouth then shut it again. Perhaps Aaloka was right this time. Tara had been thinking the exact same things that morning.

"Is there something special I should do for my visitor?" Tara asked.

Aaloka gave Tara a wide grin. "Nope. Just keep feeding it. Hummingbirds are very particular about their nectar. You will need to change it frequently, as well as carefully wash out the feeder every time. You know not to use soap though, right?"

"Of course!" Tara said, though she hadn't known at all. What, did soap kill birds?

"If you use soap, you need to just make sure that you rinse away every trace of it," Aaloka explained. "Even the smallest amount, particularly in those tiny birds, can do a lot of damage."

"I'll make sure everything's completely clean," Tara promised. Maybe she should take the feeder down and clean it tomorrow, just in case…

"Is there any chance you'll be able to walk the maze next week? Progress to the next circle?" Aaloka asked, trying to sound casual.

"No," Tara said immediately. "I'm not ready yet."

Aaloka's stare bore into Tara, as if trying to touch her soul. "You're more ready than you realize," Aaloka said firmly. "You don't have to have every spell perfectly memorized before you attempt the next step."

"But I don't want to fail," Tara admitted. "That would just be a waste of your time as well as mine. And the coven's."

Aaloka sighed visibly. "I thought that was the problem," she said. "Nothing is ever a waste. Not even failing to move from one circle to the next. I think you should try it. You would learn what you need to focus on if you do fail. And if you don't?" She shrugged and gave Tara a small smile. "You'll have succeeded. But you can't succeed unless you try."

"I'll think about it," Tara said, though she really didn't feel as though she was ready. Could she cram for the test? When would she have time? The knowledge for each circle built on the previous one. She would have to learn more qualities for all the herbs she already knew, qualities for air as well as thought. Then she'd have to learn even more, adding qualities for feeling on top of everything else.

"Truly, I think you are ready," Aaloka said quietly. "The main thing holding you back is yourself."

Tara didn't know what to say in response to that. She wasn't holding herself back, not as far as she knew. Although she did like to have everything planned out ahead of time if she did make a mistake. She tended to be very controlled, and not very spontaneous.

It was one of her personal challenges moving into the circle of wind, where storms could just blow up out of nowhere and derail her carefully formulated plans.

"Think about it," Aaloka said. "You have the

power." Then she took a step back, making Tara realize just how closely they'd moved together, talking as intimately as lovers. "I see your ride is waiting for you," Aaloka said, gesturing with her head and pointing with her chin toward Kyle. "I will see you next week. Blessed be."

"Blessed be," Tara said, bowing her head low to her teacher.

All the ride home through the comfortable silence and dark, Tara thought about what Aaloka had said to her.

Could she move forward a rank? Was she holding herself back? She just didn't know.

But maybe, on Monday, her day off, she could try a few more advanced spells. See if she could loosen up and let the winds come pouring in.

For the rest of the weekend, she was going to be far too busy between the shop and the kids.

Tara paused outside the shop Saturday morning. Weekends during the summer, particularly during nice weather, were the busiest for them with all the walk by traffic. Combine that with the solstice next week, and the internet shop was also crazy busy.

Trees dotted the street, set along the sidewalk like precise pins. They gave a little shade, which didn't help much with the heat. Cars raced along the one way street, rushing between stoplights. Both sides of the street were already full of parked cars, narrowing the passage for those trying to go about their important business. Tourists streamed by the shop, usually carrying a coffee cup or more frequently now, a cold drink.

One of the older homeless guys—Bill—had already set up a few doors down from the shop. His tanned skin looked like leather. He had a pot belly despite how skinny he looked, the ribs standing out on the sides of his naked chest. His white-and-black scraggly beard hung down just past his neck. Only tufts remained of his hair on his head, as it had receded and left an island in the center of his forehead and not much else.

For now, Bill sat quietly on the edge of the busy sidewalk with a cup out and a sign. All his worldly possessions were tightly packed around him.

Tara would have to remember to bring Bill some water later, as well as to keep an eye out for when he started ranting, usually about 1 PM. As it almost always happened at the same time every time she saw him, she figured it was when the drugs or alcohol wore off. She'd only had to call the police on him once. She hadn't wanted to, but he was scaring the customers, and she was afraid that he might hurt himself as well.

Fortunately, the homeless left the magic shop alone. They didn't have a public restroom—Tara and the others had to leave the shop and use the restroom in the warehouse building that was only accessible with a key. While it would have been easy to shoplift things from the shelves, Patricia regularly strengthened the protection spells so merchandise rarely went missing.

For a moment, Tara thought she caught a scent of the river, that watery reed smell. Then the wind changed and all she could smell was urine and sour homeless guy.

Was she finally growing an imagination? She snorted at herself. Not very likely.

She banished all thoughts of her "nightmare" man from her thoughts and entered the already busy shop.

Han Su was already there, serving someone. Patricia, too, was in the store, talking with a group of three customers while a dozen others already were browsing. Tara knew that Patricia would work the back room once Tara got settled into the front.

For most of the summer the three of them would work every weekend, at least for a few hours. The shop was closed on Mondays. Patricia handled the store by herself on Tuesdays, so both Han Su and Tara got two days off in a row.

Except for this past week with inventory, making sure they had enough supplies for solstice, so Tara had worked Monday as well.

Tara slipped her tiny backpack purse behind the counter, then brightly asked the room, "Can I help someone? Does anyone have any questions?"

The rest of the day flew by working with one person after another.

By the time four o'clock rolled around, Tara was dead on her feet, as usual. The crowds had been particularly heavy that day and she'd barely had time to gulp down the smoothie that Han Su had bought for her.

However, Tara's day was far from over. After saying goodbye, Tara raced along the crowded sidewalk, heading toward the train stop. Bill was still sitting on the edge of the sidewalk, slumped over. Maybe the meds had worked all day, as she hadn't heard him ranting when she'd brought him a bottle of water, earlier.

Or maybe it was the heat. The shop had good air flow, magically enhanced. Even on the hottest days it felt cool in there. Tara hadn't realized how hot it had actually gotten outside. Earlier in the day there'd been a lovely breeze that had kept it cooler, but that had disappeared as the sun had gained strength.

Tara remembered when Portland had had more temperate summers. The last couple of years had just gotten hotter and hotter.

Her coven poured blessings and healing into the earth, but there was only so much they could do.

Half a dozen street kids lounged near the train stop, leaning up against the brick building on the shady side of the street. One had a guitar and was strumming to himself, not really playing. They had a couple of dogs with them, of course. At least, in Portland, the street kids knew to take care of their animals. She'd heard that wasn't the case in all cities.

"Got a spare pass?" one of them asked as she walked by.

Tara just shook her head. She wanted to feel sorry for all the homeless people in the streets. However, there were just so many of them. It had gotten really bad in downtown for a while. Tara had always set up protection spells before she left her apartment, and had also bought a spray can of mace.

The new construction and gentrification had forced a lot of the homeless people out. There were still huge camps of them in most every park, near the train station, anyplace they could go.

And they rode the train. The smell of urine was so strong in the car that Tara boarded that she ended up walking to the next one just to escape it.

When Tara had been a brand new witch, she'd tried to banish such scents, trying to make where ever she was into a better place.

Wasn't that the root of all witchcraft? Or at least the modern varieties? To connect with one's location and to work to make where you lived a better place? To enrich and enliven the earth?

The problem was that despite how long people spent using public transportation, like the trains and the busses, they weren't really anyone's home. Cleaning a train car or a bus took all of Tara's strength and energy, then tied her to the location so she kept being drained.

It was a good way to burn up extra power, like after a moon ritual when she felt overly full.

But after working all day, Tara needed to recover instead of expend.

At least the train cars were airconditioned. She collapsed into her hard plastic seat and closed her eyes for a brief moment.

The smell of the river made her open her eyes again.

Just a few feet away from her, standing in front of the door, was the gentleman from last night.

He wore the same old-fashioned outfit—brown wool jacket, pants, and vest, with a bowler hat, white shirt, and string tie. His face was slightly clearer, and Tara could see that he was clean shaven. His round cheeks definitely made him look younger, maybe only in his late twenties. He had a perfectly normal nose, though she might have labeled his chin as weak.

She still couldn't see his eyes, though, couldn't tell what color they were. Were they the gray of summer storms? The blue of winter skies? Or the brown of the swollen spring waters?

He stared straight ahead, looking out the door of the train, watching the traffic and world go by.

The smell of the river rolled over Tara, as if a strong breeze had just blown off the water. Her arms suddenly felt heavy, weighed down with wet ropes. She gulped the air, struggling to take a full deep breath. Her vision grew hazy.

Just as suddenly, everything grew clear.

Dread rooted Tara to the spot. She wanted to flee, but found she still couldn't move. She could look around, and glanced this way and that, seeking a way to escape.

As the train drew slowly to a stop, the man turned to look at her. His face wavered more, as though he peered up at her from under the water.

Still, she knew, somehow, that he smiled directly at her as he tipped his hat, just before he stepped off the train.

Tara still wanted to run away, though the man had gotten off the train. It made no sense for her to get off and follow him. She stayed where she was, the fear sliding off of her as the train pulled away from the station.

Was he just in her imagination? She still wasn't sure.

She'd never heard of a ghost haunting a person and not a building or a cemetery. Despite her terror, she couldn't help but think he was human, or mostly human.

Her friend Dave would say that he presented as human, and that had to be good enough.

Why had he appeared on the train that way? Was it just to scare the crap out of her? What did he want?

And most importantly, why her?

Tara didn't know, and she suspected that she wouldn't like the answers when she did find them.

THE QUIET CLACKAMAS NEIGHBORHOOD ALWAYS reminded Tara of just how different the various parts of Portland, from the high energy streets of downtown, to the quirky, hip parts of Aurora, to the quieter, richer suburbs.

At least she could easily get to her second job on the train. It took a long while, about forty-five minutes each way. But it was cheaper to take transport than to own a car. Parking would be impossible as well where she currently lived, and yet another expense.

It took her a brisk five minute walk from the station to get to the house. The Martins had two boys, ages four and six, and needed her to come stay with them overnight most every Saturday.

Both Mr. and Mrs. Martin—Tim and Veronica— were witches. Their coven met on Saturday nights. Tara had first been recommended for the regular job from her first family, the Johnsons. When Tara had moved out of the apartment she'd shared with her then boyfriend, she'd needed a cheap place to stay. The Johnsons had taken her on as an *au pair* for their twin girls.

What Tara hadn't realized for a couple of years was that the main reason the Johnsons had hired her was because she had power. She'd stumbled into it after a couple of years, meeting Miss Lucy at one of the Johnsons' parties.

While Tara still considered the Johnsons friends, and she regularly got both birthday cards and solstice cards from the girls, she wasn't necessarily friendly with them. First of all, their economic status set them far apart from Tara who still struggled to make ends meet. In addition, they weren't the same sort of witch that she was. She wouldn't say that they practiced black magic, more like tainted.

The Martins weren't in the same coven as the Johnsons, and they practiced a more clean magic. They knew each other from their various day jobs, not their covens.

So Tara came to spend the night every Saturday night, fixing the boys dinner, spending the night, then fixing breakfast for the entire family before taking the long train ride back into the city and starting at noon at the shop again. The Martins paid very well and in cash. They didn't have to give her so much money, however, they felt as though they were paying it forward, helping a struggling new witch make ends meet.

Vicky Martin was ready by the time Tara came in the backdoor. Tim was the one who was always late. She wore a typical soccer mom outfit, a blue polo shirt over a jeans skirt, her dark brown hair tied up into a cute ponytail, with bangs over her forehead. Her white skin was always tanned, no matter what time of year.

"I'm so glad you're here!" Vicky exclaimed as she walked forward and took both of Tara's hands, squeezing them gently. "Davie has a fever. I'm sure it's nothing. But I'd like for you to prepare a healing soup for him."

"Of course," Tara said brightly, though she groaned inside. Davie was the younger boy, only four, with Carl the eldest, at six. They would normally ignore Tara all evening, coming out of their rooms for dinner then disappearing back to the games they played. (It was part of the deal they had with their parents—online games only when the parents were gone for the night, which meant every Saturday.)

If Davie wasn't feeling well, he'd want to spend all evening with her, curled up on the couch beside her. It meant he'd dictate whatever they watched on the big screen TV, then complain when she changed the channel, though he'd been asleep for the past hour.

Then again, Davie had started feeling "sick" at least once a month or so since January. Tara suspected that Davie just liked hanging out with her, but he couldn't admit that, certainly not to his parents or his brother. Girls were kind of icky, and likely to remain so for a while.

"Don't know what time we'll be home," Vickie said. "Don't worry about staying up."

Vickie always said that. Tara had only stayed up the one time, and that was because she felt as though she'd needed to talk to the boys' parents right when they got home. Carl had started a fire and Tara hadn't been sure if he'd actually used matches or not.

The boys had never shown any other indication of power, however. It was too early for any magic to manifest, though Tim had confessed that he'd had some indications when he'd been a pre-teen.

"And can you make a little extra soup?" Vickie asked as she turned away. "It's always so good."

Tara smiled. One of her strengths, both before and after she came into power, was knowing how to make food taste good with all the spices she had at hand. She'd started cooking at a young age, mainly in self-defense, because her mother hadn't been a very good cook.

Then again, her mother considered garlic an exotic spice.

"Anything else?" Tara asked as she followed Vickie out of the kitchen and into the rest of the house.

The front hallway had the front door on the left, which no one ever used, and a grand staircase that wound around to the right, enabling Vickie to make a grand entrance from time to time. Just past that was the living room. A huge, electric fireplace stood just to the right, with the big flatscreen TV hanging over the empty mantle.

A long, black microfiber couch ran across most of the room. It folded out into Tara's bed when she stayed over. Behind the couch, tall windows showed a small strip of green and a wooden fence. The air smelled of the lavender and peppermint sachet that sat in a basket on a corner of the fireplace, the heart of the home.

Davie was already curled up in a soft, beige blanket on the couch. He did look sweaty, his white skin pale, his dark eyes large in his face. Dark hair fell over his forehead and stuck up at the back of his head. He wore a green camouflage T-shirt, as well as flannel pajama pants covered in trains.

"Hi," he said softly, pushing himself up to seated.

Tara went and sat next to him on the couch, bringing the back of her hand to his forehead.

"You're a bit warm, aren't you sweetie?" she said to Davie. He wasn't running a high fever, but he was undoubtedly sick.

At least she rarely caught any bugs from anyone these days. Her own natural defenses kept her safe. Plus, if she ever did start to sniffle, she knew exactly which herbs to take in order to heal herself.

"You lay back down," Tara told Davie as she stood up. "Can I talk to you for a second?" she asked Vickie.

Vickie nodded and led the way into the formal dining room that was just off the living room. The kitchen was just around the corner, the downstairs one large circle.

"What's wrong?" Vickie asked as she stopped and leaned against the long, dark wood serving hutch.

"There's been a man, I think he's a man. He's been haunting me," Tara said. "But I don't think he's a ghost."

Both Vickie and Tim were fourth level witches.

They knew more than she did about the arcane arts and the various creatures who inhabited all the planes.

"Haunting you?" Vickie asked.

Tara told of her two run-ins with the man. She didn't like how he'd made her feel. She knew she hadn't imagined him.

Vickie listened to Tara's story carefully, nodding in sympathy. "I've never heard of anyone like that before," she said, her eyes wide. "I'll ask Tamia, our anima, if you'd like."

"Please," Tara said, nodding, relief settling across her shoulders.

"Do you think he'll show up here?" Vickie asked.

"I hadn't thought of that," she admitted. She would never knowingly put the boys in danger.

"I'll add extra protection to the house tonight, before we go," Vickie said firmly. "You'll be safe here."

"Thank you," Tara said. She wasn't sure exactly what she was going to do if this man/creature kept haunting her.

First, she needed to figure out what he was, exactly. Through knowledge came power. While a witch might have some level of wild magic, he or she could never tap into their full potential without a lot of learning and training. Or at least that was what the current schools of witchcraft believed.

Davie didn't get off the couch until after his parents had left, while Tara was already in the kitchen, starting the soup. The chicken was already in the pressure cooker, cooking, while she chopped up the herbs and vegetables she'd add next.

"Smells good," he admitted, pulling up a tall stool to sit on the counter next to her. "What's in it?"

Tara had started with a good bone broth that Vickie regularly made and kept in the freezer. "This and that," Tara teased the boy.

Davie rolled his eyes almost as well as a teenager. "What's that?" he said, pointing to her cutting board.

The large, two-inch-thick butcher block was already covered in chopped up piles of herbs. It rested over the two-basin sink on a piece of plywood that had been specifically made for just that purpose. While the rest of the house as huge, the kitchen was quite small, with very limited counter space.

"So that's lemon verbena," Tara said, pointing to the small pile in the far corner, and not what Davie was pointing at.

He merely rolled his eyes at her again. "Uh huh," he said. "And?"

Tara smiled and went through the rest of the chopped up ingredients, pleased that Davie wanted to learn.

"Thyme, rosemary, sage—those always go well with chicken," she said. Then she finally talked about the herb he was pointing to. "That's lovage," she said, handing him a small leaf. "What does that remind you of?"

He sniffed it, then took a small bite. "Celery!" he said, surprised.

"That's right," she said. "Then I have a little marjoram and some turmeric."

"That's the stuff that turns your fingers yellow," Davie complained.

"And your tongue, too," Tara told him. "You'll have to go check after dinner."

"Cool," Davie said. He watched her chop up the carrots, turnips, and butternut squash. He rested his head on his arms on the counter.

Poor boy was really sick that evening. He normally would have a bunch more questions for her and would want to help. She wasn't used to seeing him so still and quiet.

"You want to go and lay down for a while?" she asked, checking the timer on the pressure cooker. The chicken would be finished in four minutes, and she'd have to let it sit for ten more minutes, slow releasing the pressure, before she could cook the veggies.

Davie shook his head though he didn't bother to raise it.

After a bit, Tara realized that Davie was humming something. She couldn't quite figure out what it was. It seemed familiar, but not.

"Whatcha singing?" Tara asked after a bit.

"The *real* London Bridges," Davie said proudly. "Not the silly one that the other kids know."

"I don't know the real London Bridges," Tara said. "Can you teach me?"

"Sure!" Davie said. He got up off his stool, then pushed it to the side so he had a bit more room.

"London Bridge is broken down,
Dance over my Lady Lay,

London Bridge is broken down,
With a gray lady.

How shall we build it up again?
Dance over my Lady Lay,
How shall we build it up again?
With a gray lady.

Silver and gold will be stolen away,
Dance over my Lady Lay.
Wood and clay will wash away,
With a gray lady.

Iron and steel will bow and bend,
Dance over my Lady Lay.
Steel and iron will be the end,
Of a gray lady.

Build it up with stone so strong,
Dance over the dead lady.
With a heart it will last so long
From a gray lady."

Davie danced in place while he sang, circling, and sometimes lifting his arms up as children did when singing the song.

Tara turned to look at him as he ended. "Where ever did you learn that?" she asked. "I've never heard that version before."

Davie grinned at her. "Some of the boys at the daycare," he told her proudly. Then he looked worried.

"They said we weren't supposed to tell our parents, that the song was just for kids. But you're not my parent. Right?"

"That's right," Tara said. "Did those boys tell you any other secrets?" she asked, wanting to make sure that Davie wasn't getting into something over his head.

"No," Davie said, his eyes wide as he shook his head.

Tara could tell he was lying. The timer beeped at her, telling her that she should quick release the steam on the pressure cooker now.

"Thank you for singing that for me," she said. "Now, are you ready for a loud noise?"

Davie stuck his fingers in his ears and nodded.

Tara pushed the release valve, making sure that her hand wasn't in the way of the blowing steam. "Dinner will be in about fifteen minutes," she told Davie.

"Yay!" Davie said. He looked up at her. "I'm hungry," he said, as if this was something new.

"That's good. Maybe you're getting better."

Davie came over and wrapped his arms around Tara's legs, giving her a quick hug. "That's because you're here," he said. "You make me better."

"Thank you, sweetie," Tara said, patting his head. She slipped her hand down over his forehead. He seemed less warm now. "Why don't you set the table and then go get your brother?"

"Okay!" Davie said.

While the boy noisily clanked around the silverware drawer and got out bowls, Tara thought about the song he'd been singing.

It made sense to her that a song about bridges falling down would be popular with kids here—Portland had a number of bridges going across the river, plus a lot more which traversed the railroad.

Still, the song and its talk about a gray lady, a dead lady, disturbed her.

The kids didn't really understand about magic. No one would talk with them about magic unless one of them displayed that they had power.

But the term "a gray lady" was often used when describing a witch.

Was there some history in the song that Tara didn't know? And why was the song just for kids, and not for adults?

CHAPTER 3

I thought I was hardened to wilderness. I'd been born in the western territories, and have only spent the last decade in the civilized cities of the west coast. The Oregon wilderness seems different, however. Huge pines fill the forests, each so big that it would take ten men with hand outstretched to reach around a single trunk. Stands of wild rose, salmon berry, and prickly Oregon grape regularly force us from our path with their dense thorns and sharp leaves. The native I hired knows the territory, though, and keeps us on track. I hear him whispering at night to some heathen river god. I still asked him politely to teach me about the river and his beliefs. He may yet find me worthy of his confidence and his lore.

Wilson Evermore, Civil Engineer and Explorer, 1897

TARA WAS DISAPPOINTED, BUT NOT SURPRISED WHEN Vickie Martin told her in the morning that no one had ever heard of the sort of man/creature that was haunting her. However, Tara left the house in the morning with a more potent protection spell, and she carried a new sachet full of protective herbs, like heather, verbena, and tansy.

The man didn't show up at the shop either. Tara told both Patricia as well as Han Su about him, making sure that they would be prepared if he should show up.

Patricia promised to do more investigation about him. Though there were many myths about ghosts hanging around downtown Portland, particularly after the floods of the 1800s, in truth, the ghosts were very few, and none of them, at least not the real ones that Tara knew about, had died in the flood.

Still, it made sense to Tara that given the man's old-fashioned clothing, his watery nature, as well as his expressed interest in heather and bringing the rains, that he might have something to do with the floods that had plagued Portland over the decades.

When Tara got home from her long weekend of work, she still made herself take the time to strengthen all the protection spells around the condo before collapsing on her bed.

Unsurprisingly, since the man had been so much in her thoughts, he came to her in her dreams that night.

Tara found herself standing on a huge boulder. The man stood below her. She recognized him from the bowler hat still sitting on his head, though the rest of him was bare. His body was no longer human at all. Instead, he was built out of rocks haphazardly piled together, giving a hunchback shape his shoulders and making his legs bulge and move strangely.

It was still difficult for her to see his face clearly because they were both underwater, though it took her a moment to recognize that, as she had no trouble breathing. She wore a simple shift dress, reminding her of a nightgown she'd had as a child, instead of the T-shirt she'd gone to bed in.

Despite being underwater, Tara felt comfortably warm, not too hot and not too cold.

When Tara tried to step away, off the rocks, she discovered that her hands were tied behind her back. Looking around, she realized that she stood on boulders piled up around one of the piers for the Burnside Bridge, the part of the bridge that traversed from the upper part of the bridge itself, under the water, and ended buried deep beneath the river bed. She was tied to the pier. She recognized where she was from the news and the reports about the bridge repairs.

The man in front of her nodded once, then started chanting. His voice hummed low in the water, like a tug slowly making its way up the river. The chanted words echoed strangely. Sometimes they sounded clear and Tara could understand what he was saying, though the meaning slipped away as soon as she thought she grasped it. Then, other times, he made sounds like rain or like rushing water. He even echoed the cawing of seagulls and the low thump of waves on an empty hull.

Tara knew she had to escape before the man finished his circle around the footing. She struggled with the wet ropes that held her arms behind her back. She slipped, almost losing her balance. Her bare feet couldn't get a solid hold on the slimy rocks, so she couldn't kick away.

As the man continued, the smell of the water filled her nose, a spring river smell that rode high in the back of her throat, bringing back memories of cold wet winter days, when the river was swollen, pressing against its banks, threating to overflow.

"Let me go!" Tara exclaimed, surprised that she found she could talk. She struggled again with the ropes holding her, feeling them give an inch. Maybe she could slip her hands out.

She started praying loudly to Brigid, the protector of the earth, to give her the strength she needed to free herself. She asked Hayvu the goddess of the western wind to carry her away on strong winds, as well as Bonana, goddess of the water to help free her.

A strong current rushed by her at the mention of the water goddess. Tara would have been bowled over if she hadn't been held there by the ropes.

Was that the river trying to carry her away to safety? She shivered from how cold the temperature had gotten, as if the water was now trying to freeze her.

Stubbornly, Tara prayed louder to Bonana, seeking the goddess' uplifting spirit. The water around her grew colder and darker.

Maybe praying to Bonana wasn't such a good idea.

The odd man still chanted. She heard glee in his

tone. He was less than three feet from completing his circle.

Tara thanked the goddesses for listening, then started her own struggles anew. Yes, the ropes were slipping from her wrists. She couldn't quite free one hand yet, but she was close. The rope abraded her skin, and she could smell the copper of her blood, see it blooming in the water behind her back.

What could she do? She wasn't going to escape in time.

Tara remembered an old prayer about sharpening the clarity of her thoughts, bringing them to a knife point to cut away the illusions of others. The prayer was recited while making sachets of sage, lemon balm, and yes, purple heather. It had been one of the prayers that Miss Lucy had taught her.

Miss Lucy had always said that the older magick was more powerful and potent, while Sheila had insisted that the new ways were better and more reliable.

Tara had found comfort in the gentler prayers that Sheila and the others had taught her. She'd also found more power as well, or at least, her powers were more constant following Shelia's teachings.

Still, Tara started chanting the old prayer. It didn't ask for help from any god or goddess, but merely to find the strength within to withstand the illusion, to parry away falsehoods, to see clearly with her own thoughts.

The ropes loosened a touch more. Tara yanked her left hand out, then turned, took a moment to catch her balance, then started to desperately push on the rope still bound to her right.

She didn't allow herself to giggle at the thought of chewing her own hand off in order to escape. The mania might have taken over and she'd never be able to stop laughing. The echoes of her laughter in her head made her shiver.

Instead, she pushed, then pulled, folding her hand in on itself, wishing she had a real knife to cut herself free. The fingernails of her left hand broke off as she clawed at the rope. Her skin grew raw from being scratched by it, and more blood bloomed around her wrist.

She heard the man's chanting voice draw nearer. He was almost there, almost even with her, his trap complete.

With a final shove, she freed her hand. She tried to push off against the rock strongly, but her foot slipped. Still, after frantically pulling with her arms, she managed to start rising, drawing herself slowly up through the water.

She felt the moment the man completed his circle. The metal in the footing behind her rang like a dull bell, the waves echoing out, shoving her out into the darker waters.

Away from the bridge footing, the water grew so chilly Tara's teeth started chattering. Black currents raced by her, attempting to sweep her out to sea. The smell of stale water and rotten fish filled her nostrils. The water itself no longer felt clean against her bare arms and legs. Instead, it felt as slimy as rotten lettuce.

Tara wouldn't allow herself to panic. She reminded herself that she was an excellent swimmer. She stopped fighting the current and instead aimed herself upward.

How she knew which direction was up she had no idea, but she trusted her instinct. With strong strokes, she broke free of the current that had ahold of her and aimed for the spreading light that appeared above her.

As Tara's head broke the surface, she heard the man calling her name.

"Tara. Tara! You're still mine," he gloated.

With a start, Tara woke in her own room. She still shivered from the remembered cold of the water. Her wrists ached, though the skin was whole and not torn and bleeding. Her fingernails weren't broken off, though she could still feel her rapid heartbeat pulsing in the tips of her fingers, the ghost of the pain still haunting her.

Tara reached down to pull up another blanket, then realized that she was never going to sleep again, not like this. May as well make herself some tea before she tried.

Luckily, tomorrow was her day off. She would be able to sleep in.

Tara pulled her thick bathrobe out of the closet, the one that was soft and ratty and felt like it gave her a hug her every time she pulled it on. She padded silently into the kitchen—wouldn't do to wake Sharon up, who did have to work in the morning.

Without thinking, Tara reached for the herbs that would warm and soothe her, the wintergreen and rose hips. As the tea steeped she leaned over the mug and breathed in the warm humid air.

What had the dream meant? She looked again at her wrist under the light of the stove. They appeared slightly bruised. As did her fingertips, which still beat with pain.

Had she escaped from the creature? She had gotten herself untied, but she hadn't gotten away very far when he'd finished his spell. She'd still been close to the footing of the bridge.

What was he? Who was he?

Thinking about the dream, she started to remember some of the chant that the man had been saying. Each word came to her slowly as it rose out of the watery depths.

He was the Riprap man. And he would claim her soul when the light first turned to dark.

TARA SLEPT HEAVILY THE REST OF THE NIGHT, THEN HAD difficulty waking up the next morning. Still, she dragged herself out to the balcony with her tea as soon as she was able.

The day was going to be another hot one, though a cool breeze did blow in from across the river. Her plants were all doing well, and would need a good watering that morning. She'd cleaned and refilled the hummingbird feeder after Aaloka had told her not to use soap, not that it appeared to matter in the least to her little friends, as more than one hummingbird—both male and female Annas—came to visit her that morning.

Finally, when Tara felt warm all the way through to her bones, she pulled out her tablet and started doing some research. She wasn't surprised to learn that riprap was a bridge term. It referred to the large boulders and rocks placed around the footings of bridges to protect them.

She'd been standing on the riprap for the Burnside Bridge in her dream.

While there was a lot of old lore on the internet about the bridges, she couldn't find anything about the Riprap man. She did learn that the London Bridges song was ancient as well as widespread. Versions of it appeared all across Europe, in French, German, as well as Russian, though the words didn't always involve the London Bridge, just some bridge.

There were also theories about children being sacrificed to protect the bases of the bridges, or other guardians.

Just because there was no archaeological evidence—no bodies or bones had been found at the base of the London Bridge—didn't mean it hadn't happened. There were other ways of binding a soul. You didn't need to bury the body in the same place.

Tara couldn't find a direct mention of witches being sacrificed. However, had that been the true meaning of the song that Davie had been taught? Tara really wanted to know what else the boys at Davie's daycare had said, the other things he'd been taught.

Was there a song about the Riprap man?

There was just too much that Tara didn't know. After a few moments consideration, she sent off an email to Richard, asking about the Riprap man and the London Bridges song. Tara and Richard had gone on a couple of dates a few years ago, before they'd both decided that they would be better off as just friends.

A big part of their problem had been because Tara was a witch and Richard was completely mundane. There were just too many things that Tara couldn't tell him about. Miss Lucy had compared it to marrying someone from a completely different religion, which was accurate, as Tara had different gods and goddesses who she prayed to.

Plus, Richard was a research librarian. He was far too interested in any myth she mentioned, always wanting to look up things, find out more. His curiosity and his mundane nature had made it too difficult to be intimate. Tara had felt that she was lying to him all the time, even though frequently they were just lies of omission.

But Tara had held onto Richard as a friend. Almost everyone else she knew were witches or somehow involved in the community. Richard was a good reminder for Tara of the world outside, of the fact that though she mostly associated with witches and their ilk, the majority of people were mundane and without actual magic.

She checked the time. It was still before nine A.M., and a while before she could call anyone with questions. She sighed. While she really just wanted to just spend the next few hours sitting and communing with the river and her plants, she knew she had to start studying, even though it was technically her day off.

Though no one might know who this Riprap man was, Tara had no doubt that he was coming for her soul the day after the solstice, when the light began to diminish. She needed as much knowledge as she could gather before then.

～

"HELLO, SHEILA?" TARA SAID, SURPRISED THAT HER call was actually answered right away. Sheila worked as a regional manager for one of the health food grocery stores and was usually too busy to answer the phone. Tara had been prepared to leave a long voicemail.

"Hi Tara," Sheila said. "I only have a few moments between meetings. What's up?"

"There's been a man, or a creature, haunting me," Tara said. "The Riprap man. Do you know anything about him?"

"Oh, don't worry about him. He's harmless," Sheila assured her. "He'll bluster around you a bunch. He does that with the novices sometimes. But he'll fade after the solstice. You don't have anything to worry about."

"Really?" Tara asked, surprised. "He seemed pretty dangerous." She shivered in the warm morning air, remembering the dream from the night before.

"He is an odd ghost," Sheila said. "But he's just a ghost. He can't harm you."

"Wow. Are you sure?" Tara said.

"We can talk more about him at the solstice. Blessed be!" Sheila said, her end of the line going dead.

Tara sat for a moment with her phone in her hand.

Huh.

Tara wanted to feel relieved. She really wanted to believe that it had all been just a bad dream.

However, she couldn't shake the feeling that the head of her coven had just lied to her.

～

TARA WASN'T SURE WHO TO TALK WITH NEXT. SHE'D already told Patricia about the Riprap man, and she'd never heard of him. Neither had Vickie Martin, who'd asked around her coven about him as well.

Feeling guilty, Tara decided to put in a call to Aaloka and ask her. Tara didn't want to bother her teacher, but something about Sheila's response had just felt off to her.

"Blessed be," Aaloka said when she picked up. She sounded very happy to be talking with Tara. "How is my favorite soon-to-be graduated student?"

"Studying hard," Tara lied. She dragged her tablet over to her so that she could open it up to her notes as soon as she got off the phone. "Uhmmm, I hate to bother you, but I've been having some weird encounters lately."

"Really?" Aaloka said. "Like what?"

"There's been this old fashioned man who's been haunting me," Tara said. "And I had a dream about him last night. Called himself the Riprap man."

"I've never heard of anyone like that," Aaloka said.

"Are you sure?" Tara persisted. "Sheila said he comes and bothers the novices sometimes."

"Oh, that's right. Him," Aaloka said.

Tara waited for Aaloka to go on. When she didn't add anything more, Tara asked, "What can you tell me about him?" She didn't want to mention that Sheila had already told her that he was harmless. She wanted to hear it from Aaloka herself.

"Just that he appears sometimes, generally to novices. Did you talk to Sheila about him?"

"I did," Tara said. She wasn't about to lie to her teacher.

"What did Sheila tell you?" Aaloka said.

"She said that he was just a ghost, albeit an odd, threatening one," Tara admitted.

"See? He's just a ghost," Aaloka said. "You should listen to Sheila."

Tara could hear the deep sigh Aaloka took.

"But you also really need to pass to the next circle on the solstice," Aaloka said. "It's important."

"Why?" Tara asked. She felt the hairs on the back of her neck start to stand, as if a cold wind had just blown across the balcony.

"Just—trust me. It's important," Aaloka repeated. "You know I can't explain all the mysteries. Not until you're ready."

"Okay," Tara said slowly. That was a typical response—there was a lot of knowledge that remained hidden until the practitioner was ready for it. "Does passing to the next circle have anything to do with the Riprap man?"

Aaloka's tinkling laughter came across the line, sounding forced. "Of course not!" she said. "It's just important for you, for your journey."

"All right," Tara said. "I'll walk the circle of breath on the solstice." The weight of all the work she'd have to do between now and then fell heavy across her shoulders, making her bow her head.

"Good!" Aaloka said. "Then I'll let you get back to your studies. Blessed be!"

Tara hung up with her mentor and tried to straighten herself back up.

Had Aaloka also lied to her about the Riprap man? Tara had the weird sensation that her teacher had wanted to say more, but couldn't. As though Aaloka was bound by some covenant made to the coven, or to Sheila.

Tara did believe however, that Aaloka really wanted Tara to pass to the next circle on the solstice.

Would mastering breath help Tara fight a water creature? Maybe.

Tara pushed her misgivings to the side and started her studies again, trying to memorize as much as she could, unsure if any of it would help.

TARA TURNED OFF HER TABLET, THEN STRETCHED HER arms over her head and bent forward in her chair. Her brain felt overly full. Her fingers felt swollen with heat. She'd made herself an Italian soda earlier, out of chilled sparkling water, heavy cream, and pure vanilla, but it was long gone.

Even the hummingbirds who kept returning to her feeder made her weary, not delighted. The problem was that the tiny birds were very territorial, and would shoo away any other bird who dared come to feed. She'd grown tired of their constant bickering.

Nothing felt comfortable that morning, not the sleeveless shirt she wore, not her shorts, not even the ponytail she kept her hair tied up in. It pulled at odd times, tightening across her scalp like unseen fingers tugged on it.

Her mind kept circling back to what Sheila had said about the Riprap man, that he was just an odd ghost. She couldn't believe that. The dream had felt so real. When she recalled it, she could still feel the waterlogged ropes wrapped around her wrists, the slimy rock under her bare feet, how cold the waters had grown.

Normally, Tara would go for a swim to help clear her head. She wasn't afraid of the water, but she wondered if it would be a wise idea to voluntarily go someplace where she could possibly be distracted and drown.

She needed to get the truth from someone about this Riprap man. She wasn't going to ask anyone else in her coven. There was some sort of coverup happening there, starting at the highest level. She believed that Vickie Martin, when she'd asked her coven, had been told nothing. The leaders of the dozen or so covens in Portland all knew each other. If Sheila would lie to her, so would all the others.

Who else could Tara talk with? Where else could she look?

The name that came on the winds surprised her.

With a deep sigh, Tara nodded. She would listen to her wiser self, her intuition, though she didn't want to.

Miss Lucy had never lied to Tara, at least as far as

she knew. Tara had found her abrasively honest most of the time.

It was time to see if her old mentor would at least tell her the truth, if no one else would.

AFTER CALLING AND MAKING AN APPOINTMENT, TARA splurged on an Uber to get her to Miss Lucy's house. The neighborhood was in the northern part of Portland, where huge houses took up each lot with immaculate yards out front and the street full of expensive cars. Old trees lined the sidewalk, gracefully leaning over to greet their partners, providing a shaded archway along the boulevard.

Miss Lucy's house was an old craftsman, though bigger than most, and beautifully maintained. It had two stories plus an attic, as well as a finished basement and a root cellar. Miss Lucy constantly entertained there, both witches and politicians.

The left corner of the house was a round tower, complete with a witch's hat peaked roof. Tara had always thought it was delightfully ironic, as none of the witches she knew actually wore hats. The right corner was square, with tall, skinny windows on both floors, always making the rooms inside seem airy and filled with light. Gables jutted out from the attic, though Tara knew from experience that it was a dark, cobweb filled space, and that she could barely stand upright except at the very center.

Tara walked up the familiar concrete stairs from the

street to the front yard. Wild roses grew in abundance across the front of the house, stretching from the walkway to the corners. Their heady scent filled the area and their sharp thorns defended the house. Miss Lucy had woven them into her protection spells.

Gray wooden stairs led from the walkway up to the front door. Tara's footsteps sounded hollow as she walked up, as if she was walking across the deck of an empty boat. Brown wicker chairs and tables filled the front porch to the left. Miss Lucy had added a swing since the last time Tara had been here. She knew that Miss Lucy liked to spend her evenings out on the porch, sipping sweet tea as the world grew quiet.

Before Tara could knock on the door, it opened. Miss Lucy herself stood there.

Tara hadn't been certain what to expect. Though she hadn't fought with her former mentor, she'd walked away with bad feelings.

But Miss Lucy stood with a sly smile on her face and greeted Tara warmly. "Darling dear, it's lovely to see you." Miss Lucy wore dashiki shirt, made out of yellow cloth with a pattern of white, red, and black embroidered around the collar and down the front. Miss Lucy's skin coloring was a light brown, and she always wore a hat and long sleeves when she went outside so she wouldn't get any darker. She'd straightened her hair recently, wearing it short and slightly curled near her shoulders.

Miss Lucy's appearance hadn't changed much over the last few years. While she was in her sixties, she gave the impression of vibrant power, even though wrinkles lined the edges of her face and her brown eyes had faded.

"It's good to see you too," Tara said. And she wasn't lying. Miss Lucy had been such a key figure in her development as a witch. Though Tara still didn't think that Miss Lucy was following the right path, Tara still had to appreciate how much Miss Lucy had taught her.

They didn't touch, didn't hug or even air kiss. Miss Lucy had never encouraged that sort of intimacy with her students. Miss Lucy always said that she'd been raised formal, and had complained of the Victorian manners her parents had fostered on her.

"Please, come in," Miss Lucy said, stepping back to let Tara into the house. It felt cooler in here, as always. Light colored wood covered the floor, while the walls had been painted a cheery yellow. The front entranceway opened up to the large living room on the right, a spacious area where Miss Lucy entertained. Behind the closed door on the left, in the round room, was Miss Lucy's study, a comfortable place, the walls full of specially built bookcases that fit the walls perfectly.

"I was just about to make myself some tea," Miss Lucy said. A small hallway led directly from the outside door, past a small bathroom and the stairs leading to the basement, then into the kitchen. "May I offer you some?"

"Yes, please," Tara said following her mentor. She paused in the doorway of the kitchen. "You've done a lot of work here!"

Miss Lucy gave her a grin. "You don't know the half

of it. And I'm so glad it's finally finished! I didn't have a working kitchen for four solid months."

Tara nodded in sympathy. She remembered her last move and how awful everything had been until she'd finally gotten her dishes, pots, and pans unpacked so she could finally cook again.

The kitchen had been expanded greatly. Before, there had been a small sunporch just behind it. Now, the wall had been taken out and the rooms merged together. A small cooking island took up the center of the room, the entire top of it a butcher's block. Tara was already jealous of having that much space for chopping up herbs and things. Two stools were pushed up against the far side of it, allowing it to double as a cozy table.

To the left, the tiny sink had been replaced with a huge farm sink made of black slate. Would it always stay cool, even when the rest of the kitchen had warmed up? All the solid cupboard doors had been replaced with glass, making the room seem even bigger. Plus, it gave Miss Lucy the opportunity to show off her china and her crystal stemware.

The new stove was twice as large, with six burners, two on each side and a grill set in the center. Miss Lucy loved to cook and have guests over, so the large stove made sense. A huge steel hood was set above it, venting all the cooking smells outside. Tara wasn't sure how she felt about that. A kitchen should always smell of food, of garlic and steak, maybe of vinegar and fresh berries.

Miss Lucy put a bright blue enameled kettle on the stove, then selected a small white teapot with red hibiscus flowers decorating the sides. She hummed as she put various herbs into the strainer. Tara caught the scent of chamomile, lavender, and green apple. She didn't bother to ask, however. Miss Lucy would frequently make a tea, serve it to her students, then have them identify the ingredients based on taste.

When Miss Lucy had finished, she went to sit on one of the stools next to the cooking island, pulling the other out for Tara to sit on.

"Thanks," Tara said. "And thank you for agreeing to see me so quickly."

Miss Lucy nodded. "You wouldn't have called unless you were scared. Or desperate. Or both."

Tara blinked, surprised. Was she that scared? Desperate?

Or just deeply, *deeply* unnerved? As though her entire world had shifted under her feet? The last time she'd been this unsettled had been when she'd discovered that there were other paths to power, other schools of magic.

"Someone's been haunting me," Tara said. "The Riprap man."

She carefully watched her old mentor's face when she said the name. She figured talking with Miss Lucy in person was the best way to tell whether she was being lied to.

But Miss Lucy didn't try to hide her surprise, or her dismay. "That's not good," she said, shaking her head.

"What is he? Who is he?" Tara asked. Maybe she could finally get some answers.

"What have you learned so far about him?" Miss Lucy countered.

"Sheila, the head of my coven, said he was an odd ghost, but just a ghost. He'd haunt me until the solstice, then disappear," Tara admitted. "She said he was harmless."

"You don't believe her, though," Miss Lucy said. She gave Tara a smug smile.

Tara gave a sigh. She really hated feeling like a toy that Sheila and Miss Lucy both had a hold of. She'd had dreams where the various factions had actually torn her in two.

"I'm not sure if I believe her or not," Tara said stubbornly. She didn't want to go against the head of her coven, but something had been off in her conversation with Sheila. Something that had pinged hard on Tara's bullshit meter, though she couldn't say exactly what.

The kettle started whistling. Miss Lucy got up and walked to the stove. With her back deliberately turned toward Tara, Miss Lucy said, "Sheila's lying to you."

"Are you?" Tara challenged.

Miss Lucy gave Tara a sly smile over her shoulder. She shrugged. "The Riprap man isn't harmless," she said, turning serious, still showing Tara her face. "If he has targeted you, your life is in danger."

Tara swallowed against the sudden lump in her throat. She was glad that she finally had confirmation that the Riprap man was more than just a ghost.

But the fact that Sheila had lied to her…Tara didn't know what to do about that.

Miss Lucy gave Tara a few moments to sit with her thoughts while she poured the hot water into the teapot and set a small tomato timer sitting on the counter. Only then did Miss Lucy turn to face Tara again, leaning against the kitchen counter beside the stove. "There isn't much I can tell you about him," she said slowly. "I only know a few of the old tales about him. And those are all second-hand."

Tara nodded, eager to learn more.

Miss Lucy checked the clock over the stove, checking to see exactly what time it was. Then she seemed to fall into deep contemplation for a few moments.

"What is it?" Tara asked warily. She had the feeling that she wasn't going to like whatever it was that Miss Lucy was thinking about.

"There was a novice, like you, back when I was just learning the circles," Miss Lucy said slowly. "She claimed the Riprap man was haunting her. The lead witch of our coven turned her back on the poor girl. As did the rest of us."

"But why?" Tara said, bewildered. Why would her sisters and brothers turn away from a witch in need?

"Bad luck," Miss Lucy said earnestly. "As it was explained to me and the others, if we'd helped the girl, it would have brought disease, death, and destruction to all the circles. And our families as well."

"From the Riprap man?" Tara asked, confused.

Miss Lucy nodded. "Yes, as well as Mulinohana, the river god."

Was that why the waters had grown so cold when she'd started praying to Bonana in her dream?

The timer went off and Miss Lucy pulled the strainer

out of the teapot, then poured them both tea in glass cups that showed off the golden, steaming liquid.

"As I said, I can't tell you much about him," Miss Lucy said as she seated herself back on the stool beside Tara. "There are a few stories, but the living don't know much about him."

Tara picked up the cup and wrapped her cool fingers around its warmth. The scent of lemongrass and mint filled her senses. There was something warm and earthy underneath it, maybe chrysanthemum. She took a cautious sip, letting the delightful warmth seep all way into her bones.

After a moment of quiet comfort, Tara made herself ask the question that she knew Miss Lucy would want her former apprentice to ask.

"You said the living don't know much about him," Tara said. "Does that mean that there are spirits of the dead who do know more?"

Miss Lucy beamed at her former student, giving Tara the feeling that she'd just won a prize.

"Not merely dead spirits, my dear," Miss Lucy said slyly. "Dead witches."

CHAPTER 4

One by one, my companions keep falling. Old Wilkerson had to be left behind at the last village with a broken leg. The two scouts, Peter and Davis, both came down with such bad dysentery that we had to bid them farewell also. Jacob hadn't even made it much beyond Portland before a sudden cold had carried him off. Our expedition isn't cursed, despite what that old woman in the last village said to me. My native guide, Robin Goodfellow, doesn't think much about going back. He seems as determined as I am to reach our goal, following the path of the river up toward its source. He's introduced me to Mulinohana, the river god, and finally seems eager to initiate me in the mysteries now that it's just the pair of us, alone against the wilderness. I pray quietly to God that I may find the strength to continue, as

Robin leads me along deeper and darker paths, so that I might succeed in finally taming the river.

Wilson Evermore, Explorer and Initiate, 1897

TARA DID NOT MISS THE BURNING "KISS" OF THE stinging nettle, the sunbaked sour smell of foxglove, the way the poisonous sumac berries stained her fingers red. She did, however, take comfort in working beside Miss Lucy once again.

The pair of them were in Miss Lucy's studio, a small protected shack in the backyard. The shack itself had been a kit, but Miss Lucy had hired workmen to line the walls with warm maple flooring, put in cool white marble tile for the floor, and set galaxies of glowing stars across the ceiling, bright enough to light the room at night.

A long wooden workbench took up the center of the shack. Set into the center of it was a black, cast-iron cauldron, hanging over a bright blue burner (an electric heating source just wouldn't do for most potions—fire was a necessary element.)

Though the top of the workbench was a solid butcherblock, Tara still used the various chopping blocks that were hanging on the wall behind her, so that the ingredients didn't contaminate each other.

While Tara chopped and added items in the order specified by Miss Lucy, her mentor stood still, chanting and stirring, redirecting the toxins and poison of the plants into powerful magic.

Miss Lucy had laid out all the ingredients on the right side of the table, in the order that they needed to be prepared. Tara would pick them up one at a time, always circling the workbench counterclockwise, then choosing the next chopping board. She cleaned her knife between as well, using a towel that she kept slung across her shoulder.

By the time Tara reached the last ingredient—wild oregano—the smell of the concoction had shifted: instead of smelling wild and green, the air now carried the scent of a hint of summer thunderstorms and dark earth.

Tara stripped the leaves off the tall stems before she set about chopping, the sharp scent of the herb reminding her that it was getting on toward dinner time. She paused for a moment, taking a sip of water, before she continued. They couldn't stop now—the potion had to be drunk while it was still hot. If it rested, the magic would leak out.

When the leaves had been reduced to fine pieces, Tara held up the chopping board for Miss Lucy to see. She nodded, and Tara scraped the chopped up herb into the pot.

She was slightly disappointed that nothing appeared to happen when the last ingredient was added, no dramatic cloud of steam, no sudden hissing or popping.

Miss Lucy grinned at Tara's questioning look. "The oregano's just to make the potion taste better," she admitted.

"Oh!" Tara said. She was surprised. Miss Lucy generally didn't care about such niceties.

"Here," Miss Lucy said, handing the spoon to Tara.

Tara switched places with Miss Lucy, who immediately picked up her chant and started circling the table as Tara began to stir the pot. The heat had been turned down and the concoction bubbled slowly, the herbs as thick as seaweed in the river after a drought. The smell of earth intensified, though Tara still felt a lighter scent tickling the back of her throat, like rain on a summer's day.

Miss Lucy called on the familiar gods, like Brigid and Samil, along with Eural the god of the eastern wind and Areebin, the protector of souls. It had originally surprised Tara that both sects of witches prayed to the same gods, except they asked for different things. Brigid was still a protector of the earth, but Miss Lucy also asked her for permission to seek answers underground.

Tara couldn't say exactly how she knew that the spell was finished, the potion complete. Something changed in the composition of the air, though perhaps just the sense of anticipation tripled. The smell stayed the same—thickly dark with the sense of imminent storms.

Miss Lucy completed her circle and turned to Tara. "You're going to have to hurry," she said as she lifted up the caldron.

"What—I don't understand," Tara said as she watched Miss Lucy pour the brew into a waiting green-metal thermos.

"Spirits don't come to your call, willy nilly. You know that," Miss Lucy admonished as she sealed the thermos and shook it lightly once. "You need to start at the place where they are."

Tara blinked. She had known that, but she'd forgotten. It wasn't as if she was in the habit of calling up spirits. While it was possible to call a spirit or a ghost to you, the most successful rituals took place where the bodies were buried, in graveyards and watery tombs.

"Aren't you coming with me?" Tara asked as she accepted the thermos from Miss Lucy. The metal felt surprisingly cold, given how hot the mixture inside was. It also felt heavier than it should, as if the liquid inside was actually solid.

"No, I don't think I should," Miss Lucy said. She shrugged. "Bad luck."

The words stung more than the nettles had earlier. "Do you think I'll bring you bad luck? The coven?" Tara said, trying to cover her hurt.

Miss Lucy stared hard at Tara for a moment, choosing her words carefully. "If I didn't think you might have a chance, I wouldn't have helped you," she said. "But there's only so much I can do. The rest—and whether or not you survive the coming trials—is up to you."

Tara swallowed down her hurt. At least Miss Lucy probably wasn't lying to her. The coven and all the witches who were familiar with the Riprap man would consider her bad luck and wouldn't associate with her. She'd heard witches talk about the concept of luck before, but it had always been theoretical for her.

"Where do I need to go?" Tara asked as she followed Miss Lucy out of the shack. Instead of going back into the house, Miss Lucy let Tara around the side of the house, out the gate and straight out to the front.

"The bridges, of course," Miss Lucy said.

"Which bridge?" Tara asked. There were over half a dozen bridges in downtown Portland.

Miss Lucy paused at that. "Morrison," she said after a moment. "That's the oldest bridge. Go to one of the bases, near where the bridge lifts from the ground into the air. Drink the potion there and cast for the ghost of the witch who guards the bridge."

"What?" Tara said. Witches worked as protectors, yes, of local areas. But as living beings, not as ghosts or spirits.

"Quickly, now," Miss Lucy said. "You need to go. While the potion is still potent."

Tara pulled out her phone and called up an Uber. One would be there in just three minutes.

"Thank you," Tara said as she turned to say goodbye to Miss Lucy. Then, because there needed to be honest between them, she added, "I think."

Miss Lucy gave her a quick grin, unsettling and sharp. "I hope to see you after solstice," she said, setting her limits and her terms firmly. "May the spirits guide and protect you, wherever your path takes you," she added before she turned away.

A car pulled up to the house before Tara could call her former mentor back. Not that Miss Lucy would come.

Tara was on her own.

❧

TARA DIRECTED THE DRIVER TO THE EAST SIDE OF THE bridge, at Mill Ends Park, down near the waterfront. A small carnival had been set up with kiddy rides and tents for adult beverages. It was Monday night and the faire wasn't very crowded. The smell of mini donuts and spilled beer followed her as she walked past the rides, up toward the base of the bridge. Tinkling sounds of the rides swept around her.

At least the sun had finally relinquished its heat and cool breezes tickled her hair. Tara wished she'd brought a jacket with her. Then again, there might be a lot of things that she wished that night.

Standing directly under the steel girders, Tara looked up. The noise of the fast moving cars above was loud and constant. The underside of the bridge was filled with solid metal and concrete. She thought she saw the bridge sway slightly, not quickly, but in time with the traffic.

Almost like a heartbeat.

The few people visiting the faire crossed behind Tara as she faced the water. She heard them fade into the distance as she sent a quick prayer, asking for invisibility.

Her stomach turned over unpleasantly as she opened the thermos. The smell of the potion hadn't grown magically sweeter. If anything, the scent of the liquid mingled with the smell of the dirt under her feet and the scent of stale water in front of her.

Would Miss Lucy poison her? Tara doubted it. First off, if Miss Lucy was angry with Tara, she wouldn't hide it, she'd speak her rage to the person directly.

Of course, there were always accidents, with potions not precisely measured out, ingredients being substituted or not the highest quality, the proper prayers not being applied.

And sometimes it was just the will of the gods.

Tara took a deep breath through her mouth, trying to calm her twisting stomach. But no relief came.

Closing her eyes and asking again for blessings, Tara lifted the potion to her mouth.

The first mouthful was like warm sludge. It tasted like dirt—no, compost. Dirt that at one point had been shit. Then the bitterness spiked through her, awful and insistent, coating the top of her mouth. And that was after Miss Lucy had added the wild oregano to make it taste better?

Tara forced herself to swallow. She gave an entire body shudder. She did *not* want to drink any more of the vial potion.

She had no choice.

Lifting the thermos again, Tara opened her mouth and took another swallow. This one was both better and worse. It still tasted like dirt, but now, instead of bitterness came the slime of rotten cabbage. Tara made herself swallow, feeling as though worms now crawled down her throat.

Tara gritted her teeth and sucked in air, willing herself not to vomit. Her head pounded with sudden heat. Her hand grew clammy at the same time. She swayed, but she would not stop.

Her hand raised the flask. It took effort for Tara to

unlock her jaw. Just one more swallow was all she had to manage. Then she could start her call.

The oregano rode on the top of the vile substance this time, like a savory coating on a rotting piece of meat. Tara couldn't help but start hacking even as she forced the liquid down. Her eyes watered and she couldn't breathe for a few moments. She found herself bent over, one hand on her knees while the other still cradled the precious potion.

Finally, Tara recovered enough of herself to seal the thermos back up. The smell remained. It had transferred to her throat, her hair, her hands. Even her tears.

It took two tries for Tara to clear her throat enough to utter the first words of the calling, entreating Brigid to welcome her into the embrace of the earth, to guide her to those who lived there, to protect her steps and lead her back to the light.

Tara's heart pounded more and more slowly. She felt herself falling into a trance. She couldn't help but sway where she stood. She knew the people passing behind her, though who could actually see her, probably thought she was drunk.

Dark spots formed on the ground before Tara. She blinked, trying to clear her vision.

It took her a few moments to realize that the dark spots were growing, solidifying into a single great maw.

Tara bit back her screams as she felt herself falling forward, a terrifying dark mass yanking her off her feet.

Down.

And into the very earth itself.

TARA HAD ASSUMED THAT CALLING A WITCH'S SPIRIT would be similar to calling a regular spirit. That despite the drama of the dark hole and the horrible potion, that a ghost would appear beside Tara underneath the bridge.

It never occurred to her that the ghost would draw Tara's spirit down to its residence, instead.

The room was sparsely furnished. A red couch pushed against the wall, with gold cushions, looking like a comfortable place to curl up with a good book. A tall fireplace with a roaring fire stood opposite the couch, the old-fashioned mantle made from river rock, all nubby and gray. The fire burned with bright blue flames, and no heat, as though it was merely an illusion. The walls looked like rock carved with a melon baller, scooped out one foot at a time, with hard ridges at the edge of every hollow. She would have to remember to never rest her hand or brush against them—they looked uncomfortably sharp. A large braided rug covered much of the floor, but it couldn't hide the fact that it was still plain, beaten dirt everywhere.

To the left of the couch stood a closed wooden door. Before Tara could call out, the door opened.

"What do you want?" said the woman who came steaming out. She looked so perfectly put together that Tara wondered if she was a model.

Her black hair was done in a poodle cut, a 1950s style, with tight curls in the front and pulled back along the sides with glittering ruby-encrusted pins. Dark pencil emphasized her almond-shaped eyes, which were a brilliant emerald color. A slight bit of rouge pinked-up her white cheeks and pale lips, making her look young and fresh. Her face was heart-shaped, with a broad forehead, slightly thinner cheeks, leading down to a pointed chin. Though she had a tiny nose, Tara would bet that the woman constantly was sticking it into other people's business.

The woman wore a light blue shirt dress with a white collar, also very 1950s, white cuffs around the short sleeves, and tiny white buttons down the front. It looked both comfortable and stylish. A tight black belt showed off her tiny waist. She had on black pointed shoes with kitten heels, as well as nylons. Only the shoes looked out of date—or perhaps they just hadn't come back into style yet.

"Who are you?" the woman asked, pulling up sharply when she saw Tara.

"My name's Tara," she said. "I called on the spirit of the witch who guards the Morrison Bridge."

The woman nodded. "I am she. Dorothy Parkerson. Welcome to my prison, or as I like to call it, cell sweet cell. Why are you here?"

Tara paused, at a loss. "I am being hunted by the Riprap man," she confessed.

"How did you have the power to come down here?" Dorothy said. Her perfectly plucked eyebrows scrunched together across her forehead, showing her complete puzzlement.

Though Tara was still learning to see, she could sometimes catch a glimpse of another's power and be able to gage their strength. She assumed that Dorothy could read her, and had realized that Tara didn't have the power to make it down to the "cell sweet cell" on her own.

"My former mentor gave me a potion," Tara said. She looked down. The thermos was nowhere to be seen. Though she was still wearing the same T-shirt and shorts, and she felt solid enough when she reached over with one hand to squeeze her other, she doubted she was actually there, in the flesh. Her body was probably still somewhere else, either in a daze or passed out. As she'd been in a public space, she really didn't have much time before someone called 911.

Dorothy reached out and tried to touch Tara. Her hand passed uncomfortably through Tara's arm, casting spikes of cold through Tara's bones.

"Sorry," Dorothy said.

"It's all right," Tara told her. "What can you tell me about the Riprap man?"

"He caught me," Dorothy said, her thin lips pressed together into a pretty scowl. "Same as he's caught all of us."

"Us?" Tara asked. "There are more of you?"

"One for each bridge," Dorothy said, nodding. "We've formed our own coven," she added. "I'd thought you were the Burnside Bridge witch, coming to complain about the construction again." She paused, then added, "Tell me, what level are you?"

"First level initiate," Tara said. "I'm in the first circle, head, or thought."

"How close are you to the second?" Dorothy asked.

Tara shrugged. "My teacher wants me to try for the second level on the solstice, in two days' time."

"You have to make it," Dorothy told her fiercely. "We—all of us—were only first level initiates when the Riprap man came calling for us. I don't know if a second level practitioner could escape him or not."

"Thank you," Tara said. For the first time in a day, she felt a touch of relief overcoming her constant sense of dread. Maybe she could pull herself out of his grasp.

"What else can you tell me about him? Who is he?" Tara asked. A wave of dizziness washed over her. Her body was demanding her spirit's return.

"You know what riprap is, yes? The boulders piled around the pier of a bridge?" Dorothy said.

"Yes," Tara said.

"Riprap protects the bridges from waters and flood. The Riprap man captures witches as well, taking our hearts and drowning us in the river, sacrificing us on the riprap. Then he binds each soul to a bridge."

"How?" Tara asked. She spread her fingers wide, then made claws of her hands, trying to keep herself in Dorothy's living room for just a few moments longer.

"Dark magic. Black magic. Old magic," Dorothy said. "The Riprap man works for the old god of the river, who doesn't like witches. Some old feud that no one suspected or remembered."

"Why is he coming for me?" Tara said. The room wavered, but she grit her teeth and consciously remembered the awful potion that she'd drunk, just to get here.

Dorothy sighed. "The Burnside Bridge is being repaired, isn't it?"

Tara nodded. She'd been keeping track of the progress on the website. There was structural damage, steel inside the concrete footings that needed to be replaced.

"The Riprap man always needs a new witch when there's work being done. I'm the third Morrison bridge witch. The others have passed."

Tara shook her head. Not only would the Riprap man drown her in the river and then bind her to a bridge, the existing witch would be snuffed out of existence. It wasn't necessarily a good or nice existence, but still.

"He'll come for you at midnight, the day after the solstice, when the dark starts to retake the light," Dorothy warned. Her voice grew faint. "Move to the second level. That may save you when the Riprap man comes calling."

"Thank you," Tara whispered. "Blessings on you," she added, though she didn't know if Dorothy heard her or not.

Tara rose rapidly through the earth, her spirit returning to her body causing an upheaval. She bent in half and heaved, throwing up the potion. It splashed at her feet, vile and green. Long worms—or maybe just living bits of herbs, twisted together—squirmed in the vomit before sinking back down into the earth.

No one seemed to have noticed her momentary lapse. How long had she been absent? Maybe five minutes, not much more. At least she'd been able to keep to her feet and hadn't fallen over.

A couple of men passed by as Tara wrapped her arms around her stomach, holding herself. She could tell from their sharp looks that they were assessing whether or not she was worth the effort—was she out of it enough that she wouldn't put up too much of a fight? Or was she too much work? Would she keep vomiting instead?

With a shaky hand, Tara reached down and picked up the mostly empty thermos. It was to her side, away from the stinking pile of puke. Then she stood up straight and stared at the men. Hard, her "don't fuck with me" face firmly set.

The two men wisely moved on, though Tara hoped they wouldn't find a target.

With shaky legs, Tara started to make her way back out to the street. Her mouth tasted like she'd been on a three-day bender. She couldn't wait to get back to her apartment and brush her teeth. Maybe even twice.

Then, Tara was going to have to make herself a large pot of caffeinated tea. Strong enough to keep her awake through the night. And into the next day as well.

She had to spend every hour that she could studying over the next couple of days so that she might pass into the next circle, out of reach of the Riprap man.

TARA RUBBED AND BLINKED HER EYES, TRYING TO clear the crud from them. She gazed blearily at her alarm clock. She'd been up past two A.M., trying to cram in as much knowledge as she could. The alarm told her that it was now seven.

She could survive on four hours of sleep, right?

Shaking her head, Tara pushed herself up to sitting. She yawned and stretched her arms over her head, trying to wake up. She'd never been much of a morning person. It took her a couple of hours to get herself moving after she woke up.

But she had no choice. One last day of studying and practicing before tomorrow, the solstice. The coven wouldn't meet until after dark, however, Tara had to work all day. She might be able to get Han Su to cover for her, except that she'd already asked for the afternoon off on Wednesdays, due to her new class schedule. And Patricia would be too busy with her own coven and preparing for solstice.

Tara padded off to take a shower, turning the water extremely warm, hoping it help wake her up. She didn't stay under the spray for as long as she would have liked: something about how hypnotic the falling water was had her swaying on her feet.

She cursed the Riprap man once again. Water was Tara's element. She loved swimming, boating, fishing, anything to do with the water. She'd chosen this apartment specifically because it was so close to the river.

Now, she was looking at all things connected with water with a cautious eye.

She couldn't wait for this to be over, so that she could get on with her life. In some sense or another.

After she'd made her tea—a green tea with marigold

flowers, lavender, hyssop, and a touch of cinnamon—Tara sat on her balcony and breathed in the morning. She heard Sharon rummaging around behind her, making her usual English muffin with fake butter and artificially sweetened jam.

If only the rent wasn't so expensive here! Tara loved this apartment. But she needed someone like Sharon who could pay for more than half of the rent.

The little Anna came thrumming by, circling to make sure no rival was near before he—no, she, as there was no red on the head or chest—settled down to take a few sips.

"I hate those things," Sharon said as she walked out onto the balcony, clunking down her plate and cup.

"Hate?" Tara had to ask.

"It's unnatural how they move," Sharon said. "They flit around so fast, then just hoover. And they're aggressive. They divebomb me every time I come out here."

"Maybe they just don't like you in return," Tara said. She blinked, then swallowed. She was too tired for polite conversation just then, and was going to get herself into trouble with Sharon by speaking her mind.

"Like you," Sharon said, looking out over the edge of the balcony. "You don't like me much, either."

Tara didn't know what to say. This was the worst time for her to be trying to have this sort of heart-to-heart conversation with her flatmate.

"It's okay," Sharon said. "We don't really fit well together. We're like oil and water."

"Yeah, we kind of are," Tara said with a sigh. She

knew what was coming.

"Our lease will be up at the end of next month. If you want to stay here, and I think you love this place so much more than I do, you're going to need to find a new flatmate," Sharon said. "I'll be moving out."

The blow hit Tara hard in the center of her chest. For a moment she couldn't take a deep breath. Finally, she swallowed down her disappointment and said, "Thank you for giving me so much notice."

"I'm not an asshole," Sharon said, glaring at Tara.

Tara was glad that she was able to keep her lips pressed together and not reply.

Though possibly she didn't do as good of a job of keeping her thoughts to herself as Sharon added, "No matter how much you might consider me one."

"I'm sorry," Tara said immediately.

Sharon shook her head. "As I said, we just don't get along. I don't think it's either you or me." She paused, then added, "And it's true that you probably bring out the worst in me. Just like I bring out the worst in you."

"I'm not going to deny it," Tara said after a moment, as this appeared to be a morning of truths. "I really wish you the best," she said.

"And I wish you the best with all your studies and like that," Sharon said.

Tara had given Sharon the lie that she was taking an online course, hoping to become a registered herbalist.

They spent the rest of the time before Sharon got up to leave in a more-or-less comfortable silence, watching the river flow beneath them, changing but not changing as always.

AFTER SHARON HAD GONE TO WORK FOR THE DAY, TARA checked her email, pleased to find a note from Richard, her friend the research librarian.

In it, he gave her a long, scholarly text about London Bridges, which she merely scanned. No mention of the gray lady in anything he could find.

What caught her attention was that he'd found a fragment of a child's song that did mention the Riprap man.

Oh, the Riprap man will build it tall
Start out small
Oh, the Riprap man will build it tall
Start out small

Roll the boulders like balls
Start out small
Roll the boulders like balls
Start out small

Lift them up like a great wall
Start out small
Lift them up like a great wall
Start out small

Oh gray lady can you resist the call
Start out small
Oh gray lady can you resist the call
Start out small

Richard had included both a recording played on a flute as well as the sheet music. It had a simple tune, like London Bridges. He theorized that it came with a game, like London Bridges, with children squatting down every time they sang the chorus of "Start out small."

Instead of replying, Tara picked up the phone to call Richard.

"Good morning," Richard said, answering the phone.

His warm voice made her smile. It really was a shame that they just weren't compatible. Plus, Richard had recently started dating a very nice woman who Tara approved of. She wanted him to be happy.

"Good morning," Tara said. "Thank you so much for the work you did."

"My pleasure," Richard said. "Seriously. If there's ever anything you need for me to look up, just let me know. It's summer, and I have a lot of time on my hands."

"I may," Tara said slowly. "I'm actually looking into an ancestor," she lied. Well, sort of. All witches were family in one way or another, right? "Her name was Dorothy Parkerson. She disappeared in the late 50s, like 1957, 1958, sometime around then."

Tara didn't want to give the specific date, as she wasn't sure if Dorothy would have been sacrificed before the bridge was complete or afterward.

Just as the Riprap man was coming for her before the bridge construction was finished.

"You got it," Richard said. "I'll see what I can find. I

supposed you're going to a big party tomorrow night, right?"

"Yes," Tara said warily.

Richard laughed. "It's okay. You tend to celebrate the solstices, as well as the equinoxes."

"Oh. Right," Tara said. She guessed that was obvious.

"How are your studies going?" Richard asked.

"Fine," Tara said. "But speaking of such…"

"Okay, okay, I can take a hint. Lots on your plate right now. Give me a call after the solstice, all right?"

"I will," Tara promised. She hesitated. How much could she tell Richard? What could she tell him? "You've always been such a good friend," she added. "I have always appreciated you. Thank you."

"You're welcome," Richard said. "I appreciate you as a friend too. And…well, I'd like to talk with my friend about Lisa, soon."

Tara blinked, taking a few moments before she remembered that Lisa was the woman Richard was currently dating. "Getting serious?" she asked.

"It is," Richard said. "It's really weird and wonderful and exciting and it isn't scary, which is the weird part."

"I can't wait to hear all about it," Tara told him sincerely. "I'm happy for you."

"Thank you," Richard said. "You don't know how rare that is, for a friend to be supportive of another friend's good luck."

"You got the wrong friends, then," Tara said. Damn

it! She really needed to not actually talk with anyone while she was so tired.

But Richard just laughed. "Yup," he said. "Which is why I appreciate you as a friend."

"Thank you," Tara said. It was good to know that at least someone in her life wasn't lying to her.

"I'll send you any information I can find on Dorothy," Richard added. "Talk with you soon."

"Thanks, bye," Tara said.

She sat for a while, bemused at how her life seemed to be turning out.

The witches she'd known and trusted, her teachers and her mentors, were possibly not as good as she'd once believed. And the other people in her life, the mundanes, were turning out to be better.

TARA FOCUSED ALL HER ENERGY BETWEEN HER HANDS and the whirling ball of winds contained there. It was a more advanced spell, to control and capture the winds, rather than just call on them and direct them to blow here or there.

Now, she just had to push her hands out, away from her chest. It felt as though she carried a heavy medicine ball, like what they had at the gym. Except that this challenged both her physical as well as her mental powers, the ball growing heavier as she pushed it away from the center of her being.

The next part was to be able to stand with the ball.

Tara tightened the muscles in her thighs, preparing herself to slowly rise from her chair.

She was doing it! Rising up! It took so much concentration to be able to do two things at once, such as carry on a spell and walk. Much harder than patting your head while rubbing your stomach. More like performing a handstand on a unicycle and reaching down with one hand to spin the pedals while at the same time juggling fireballs with your feet.

A shrill bell rang. Damn it! Tara had forgotten to mute her phone. Her concentration broke. The ball blew apart, the winds rushing away from her. A couple tried to push through her out of spite, angry that they'd been contained even for a little while.

Tara sat back down, her legs and arms shaking.

The phone continued to ring. Tara slid it over towards her, then sighed.

It was her mom. Time for their weekly mother-daughter chat.

"Hey Mom," Tara said as she answered.

"Hello," Mom replied. "What are you up to?"

"Studying," Tara said honestly. "Got a big test tomorrow." All of which was factually true. "How are you? What are you and Dad up to this week?"

Tara had grown up in Menomonee, Wisconsin. It was situated about halfway between two large cities, the Minneapolis/St. Paul twin cities to the west, and Madison to the east and south. Tara had never felt as though she'd belonged there. There wasn't much there to start with, as Menomonee wasn't that big of a town. Plus, she'd grown up pretty close to the freeway, and always felt as though she needed to go, to travel, caught between two big magnets, never sure which direction was right.

It was part of why she'd followed Sean out to the coast. A part of her had known exactly how irresponsible it was for her to move halfway across country just to be with a boy. However, she'd needed the excuse to get out of Wisconsin and somewhere else.

When Sean had broken up with her, it had been devastating at first. Tara hadn't known anyone, hadn't found a job yet, didn't have any money. She'd been looking at either having to live in the street or return home with her tail between her legs. Both options had about the same appeal.

Then she'd answered an ad for an *au pair* job, that would give her both food as well as a place to stay. Though she didn't have any experience beyond taking care of her two younger siblings, the Andersons had hired her right away.

Tara hadn't learned until years later that the Andersons had recognized that Tara had a spark of power. It had taken Tara five years to realize what she had and to start working with it. Which had led to Miss Lucy and everything else.

Tara's mom and dad, as well as her younger sister and brother, had all stayed in Wisconsin. Tara tried to make it back for Christmas every year, frequently traveling on the actual holiday, as she'd had her own celebration on the solstice with her newly acquired family just before.

Tara's parents had started raising their family late,

and so were now retired. They'd bought a hobby farm north of town, a fixer-upper. It had surprised Tara how much both of her parents had bloomed in the country, taking classes and watching YouTube videos about home repair, doing much of the work themselves now.

"We're working on the pumphouse," Mom said. "The roof started leaking this winter, probably the weight of all the snow on it. So we're having to replace that."

"What does that entail?" Tara asked. She was endlessly curious about all the handy things that her parents now did, things they would have hired someone to do when she'd been growing up.

"First, we have to remove all the shingles and tarpaper covering the roof," her mom explained. "Then remove the deck—the actual plywood making up the roof itself. Replace it, put some good tar on it to seal it fully, then put back on tarpaper and shingles."

"Wow," Tara said. "Sounds like a lot of work. You be careful on those ladders, you hear?" That was the last thing that Tara needed right now, was for one of her elderly parents to fall off the roof.

Mom laughed, a warm sound. "That's exactly what I've been telling Henry," she said. "I'll be sure to let him know that his daughter is worried as well."

"Good," Tara said. "But you be careful as well."

"Oh, I am. Trust me," Mom said. "And the fact that if Henry falls, I get six months of *I told you so*, is a true caution for him. And for me as well."

Tara smiled. Her parents made bargains and bets with each other all the time. The payment was frequently limited bragging rights, for a day up to six months, but no longer than that. Sometimes the payoff would be dishwashing duties, doing the laundry, washing floors, general clean up, and so on.

"I'm glad to hear that you're both being cautious," Tara said. It would be difficult to do a long-distance healing, but she'd try if either of her parents were injured.

"So tell me what you've learned this week," Mom said. She was also interested in plants and wildlife, particularly since moving to the farm. She was even learning a little herbal lore and had started drying berries and herbs to make her own teas.

"I learned about London Bridges," Tara said instead of sharing more about herbs. "How the children's song spread all the way across Europe."

"Interesting!" Mom said. "Was that because Portland has so many bridges?"

"Exactly," Tara said. A lump suddenly formed in Tara's throat. "Mom, you know that I love you and Dad and the brat and Timmy, right?"

"We do," Mom said. "Why? What's wrong?"

"I just…it's everything," Tara confessed. She blinked her eyes, trying to keep back the tears. "Some of my friends—they're not who I thought they were." Particularly Sheila, the head of her coven, who had lied to her about the Riprap man, who hadn't tried to help her.

Mom's sigh echoed in Tara's ear. "I'm sorry," she said. "Is there anything we can do to help?"

"No," Tara said, shaking her head. "I wish there

was."

Tara heard yelling in the background.

Her mom obviously put her hand over the phone, trying to muffle her shout of, "I'll be right there!" Then she returned to Tara. "Henry says that break's over," her mom said, the amusement apparent. "I keep telling him that we don't have to finish this in one day, but he still thinks he's eighteen or something."

That seemed exactly like her dad, always convinced that he was invincible.

"Tell him that I love him too," Tara said. Damn it. How could she say goodbye to her mom without raising all her motherly instincts and suspicions?

"I will. You want me to call tomorrow?" Mom asked.

"Maybe?" Tara said, hating how her voice quavered.

"I will, then," Mom said. "I'll write it down in my calendar."

More shouting occurred in the background.

"I know, you have to go," Tara said before her mom could say anything else. "I'll talk with you tomorrow, okay?"

"Okay. Love you bye," Mom said, hanging up.

"Love you bye."

Tara slowly lowered the phone back to the table. She couldn't say much more to her parents about what was going on. How badly would it destroy them if she was killed? They'd be devastated.

But she couldn't prepare them for that.

All she could do was to study, even harder, so that she didn't end up disappointing them by dying.

CHAPTER 5

I would never have believed it if I hadn't seen it for myself. I've always been a man of science, an engineer. Magic was only for old-wives' tales and uncultured natives. How little did I know! I castigate myself daily for my ignorance. How much more could I have done, how great would be the bridges my company builds, using magic! However, I understand the caution that Robin employs. Too much of this power in the wrong hands could be disastrous. He's shown me, himself, what happens when a witch's coven meets, the harm they cause to the land as well as to their fellow man. It isn't our place to stop them, however. We are close to the river's source, the power all around us. When we get there, we will call forth the gods to see if we can strike a bargain with them, to protect

the eggshell fragile towns and cities strung along the water like pearls.

Wilson Evermore, Initiate and Beginning Magician, 1898

TARA DRAGGED HERSELF TO "YE OLDE MAGICK Shoppe" Wednesday morning, the day of the solstice. Her head felt overly full of knowledge, her bones creaked with suppressed magic, ice dragging itself through her blood, the winds still whispering in her ears.

For all her focus on air and wind, Tara had tried not to forget that the essence of this circle was actually breath. Not just the winds and the breath of the world, but the breath of the body as well. She knew that she hadn't studied as much of the internal art as much as she probably should have. Hopefully the shop would be quiet that day and she'd have a chance to meditate and work on her breathing.

However, there were already a couple of people standing outside the shop when Tara arrived, fifteen minutes before the door was supposed to be open. "I'll let you in at ten," she promised the two women as she unlocked the door.

"Take your time, hon," the one said, with a wave of her hand. "It's nice enough out here this morning."

Her friend looked askance, but Tara didn't ask.

"Thank you," she said, slipping inside the shop and locking the door behind her.

At least everything looked normal enough.

She didn't care for the smell of the river that rose up as soon as she stepped into the backroom, sliding her lunch and dinner into one of the refrigerators there.

Quickly, Tara went back into the main room. She counted the money in the register as fast as she could, totaling the bills up, making sure that it agreed with the count from the night before, then she opened up the door to customers five minutes before the store was officially supposed to open.

Tara tried to focus and study the few times the shop had a lull. However, every time she was alone, her sense of dread overwhelmed her. The smell of the river kept haunting her.

Damn it! She kept trying to remind herself that she loved the water, loved living on the river. Now, she wondered if she'd ever be able to look at it the same.

The shop closed up early that night, as it was considered one of the major holidays. When Tara texted Kyle, he agreed to come and fetch her for the meeting that night.

"So, how's your nightmare man?" Kyle asked as Tara started closing up the shop. He wore a gray T-shirt with a beige vest and blue jeans, looking very stylish.

"Don't think you want to know," Tara said. She wasn't sure if she wanted to tell Kyle anything about the Riprap man.

"Why is that?" Kyle asked, the surprise at her answer masking what was sure to be some hurt.

"Honestly? It's so that you have deniability," Tara said. "I don't want to bring you trouble. And you may have some, if I told you anything." Tara really didn't want Sheila or the others declaring Kyle bad luck. He needed the coven, needed a family he could declare his own.

Kyle stood in the center of the shop, mulling over what she'd just said. Finally, he turned and walked over to the door of the shop, planting himself just in front of it, arms crossed over his chest. He went so still he looked like a guardian carved out of black marble.

"I think you're wrong," Kyle said solemnly. "Now, you know that I've gone through some bad shit," he said after a few moments. "The only way I got through that was with the help of some very good friends. So this not telling me for my own good bullshit? Is just that. Bullshit. Tell me."

"Kyle, I—"

"Tell me. Now," Kyle said. "Or I'll make sure you miss this meeting."

Tara blinked, surprised. She wasn't sure where exactly this was coming from.

"This nightmare man got you spooked," Kyle said. "He been chasing after you. You need help. I don't leave my friends, and particularly not my good friends, to go hang in the wind."

"It really isn't smart—"

"Don't care," Kyle said. He lifted his chin, looking even more stubborn than he had. "Tell me."

"Sheila and the others will deny what I tell you," Tara said, stalling. "And they might decide that you're bad luck as well."

"If it weren't for bad luck, I wouldn't have no luck at all," Kyle said with a ghost of a smile. "So tell me."

So Tara told Kyle everything she knew about the Riprap man, how he'd been haunting her, why he was probably coming for her. About visiting Miss Lucy to get the potion, as well as Dorothy.

Kyle didn't move until Tara was finished.

"All right then," Kyle said. "We got a plan. You need to pass your test tonight."

"Yes," Tara said. "So can we get going?"

Kyle gave her a sheepish grin. "Sure, sure. But I'm going to grill you all the way out. And tell you about what happened to me passing the circles."

"Will that help?" Tara asked. As far as she knew, though witches all passed through the same circles, each initiation was different.

Kyle shrugged. "Won't hurt to know a bit more about the process before you start. Now, you ready finally?"

Tara rolled her eyes at him. "Yes, I am."

"Then let's get you out to the meeting. And get you past that test."

AALOKA WAITED FOR TARA INSIDE THE HOUSE, IN THE pantry next to the kitchen. Candles stuck up from every surface, giving the room a warm glow. The pantry was square at the back end, sloping to a point at the front, where a window box had been built, the shelves full of herbs. Tara smiled at the greenery. Even in the dim light, she recognized most of them: basil, sage, coriander, sorrel, oregano, and hyssop, to name a few.

"I passed forward your application to move between the circles tonight," Aaloka said. She held out her hands, drawing Tara closer. "I must admit, I was surprised at the resistance I got from Sheila."

Tara swallowed hard against a suddenly dry throat. "Did she refuse to let me walk the maze?" Tara hadn't even considered that the head of her order might block her that way.

Then again, Sheila had lied to Tara about the Riprap man.

What would happen to the coven if the Riprap man didn't claim his sacrifice? Would they fall under "bad luck", as Miss Lucy had described?

"She pushed back, but there were several of us who spoke up on your behalf," Aaloka said. "So you will be walking the maze, trying to pass from the circle of thought to the circle of breath."

"Thank you," Tara said, squeezing Aaloka's hands briefly. Her head was suddenly light. The candles seemed much brighter now. She made herself take a deep breath, widening her stance to steady herself.

"What do I need to do?" Tara asked. She'd had to pass an oral exam when she'd first passed fully into the first circle, then the "practicum" of walking the meditation maze. Kyle had said that had been his experience as well. Tara still thought she should ask.

"It will be much the same as the first circle," Aaloka told her. "First, an oral exam, which I'm sure you'll pass. Then, the walk." Aaloka sighed. "Just keep your head on straight, your thoughts clear, and I'm sure you'll make it."

"Thank you," Tara said. "What else can you tell me—"

"Tara?" One of the existing initiates of breath, a fair-haired, willowy woman named June, poked her head into the pantry. "It's time for you to be prepared."

"Blessed be," Aaloka said, bringing her palms together and bowing her head to Tara.

Tara returned the gesture, then followed June out of the pantry, through the house and into the sunroom at the back, overlooking the garden. The other initiate of breath, Wren, was already standing there.

The room itself was comfortable, longer than it was wide, with couches on the long walls and overstuffed chairs on the shorter ones. Windows filled three of the walls, the fourth being the actual outside wall of the house. The sunroom had obviously been added to the house later, probably in the 1970s.

Just outside of the room stood Sheila and the others who were in the upper circles. They stood motionless, holding candles, obviously there to judge her performance.

Tara felt her back stiffen and her chin come up. She could do this.

"You need to be purified for the ceremony," June said. "You'll have to first change clothes."

It was only then that Tara realized that both June and Wren were dressed in long white gowns, lightweight and gauzy.

Tara looked at the pair of them, refusing to glance at the observers. The pair standing in front of her obviously expected her to strip bare here and now.

That was different than the first time, or than what Kyle told her. Then again, Kyle was a man with a badly abused psyche. They might not have insisted that he strip nude in front of everyone.

But Tara slipped her T-shirt over her head, then kicked off her sandals, jeans, then her bra and panties. She stood before the everyone with her head held tall, not trying to cover up her body. She might have a little extra weight than she was officially supposed to have according to society, and had a soft belly, but she also had curves, hips, and a great tits.

"Good," June told her with a smile. "You keep your head up."

Was this part of the test? If Tara had balked, would she have failed before she'd even started?

June and Wren rubbed scented oils into Tara's skin, starting at her neck and working their way down. It smelled sweet, of myrrh and lavender. Her head started buzzing as they finished. She took a deep breath. Was it just caffeine? Or was it magic? She couldn't tell.

"Put this on," Wren said, handing Tara a robe. It was white with green leaves embroidered along the front of it, around the collar and the cuffs. "You'll take this off when it's time to walk the maze," Wren added.

"Thank you for beginning my initiation," Tara said, nodding to both of them. "Blessed be."

"Blessed be," they intoned in unison. "Now, you

need to stay here for a bit while your teacher comes to test you."

Tara nodded and widened her stance, prepared to stand for the entire ordeal.

"Glad to see you're prepared," June said with a smile. "I look forward to welcoming you to our circle."

Tara puzzled over the looks and expectations that the two initiates of the circle of breath had seemed to already have. Had someone "warned" them about Tara? How she might not actually be ready?

Aaloka came into the sunroom next. She'd changed clothes as well, and now wore a midnight blue sari with a glittering starburst pattern woven into the cloth. Her black hair was tied back into its usual bun, and a sprig of jasmine was pinned to the top of it. A sparkling red jewel had been pasted to the center of Aaloka's forehead, and her red lipstick matched.

"Though you are my student, I will not go easy on you," Aaloka warned as she rested the book she was carrying on the closest end table. "Tell me, what are the medicinal properties for *rhamnus purshiana*?"

Tara smiled. Kyle had been drilling her the exact same way during the drive out.

This part, she knew. Though her brain might have still felt overly full from everything she'd tried to cram into it the last couple of days, Tara knew that she could remember the important parts concerning herbs and lore.

It was the practicum that concerned her. Particularly since she'd have to overcome magic of some of the others.

Would Sheila be there? Tara wasn't strong enough to take on the head of the coven.

However, Tara was determined to successfully walk the circle tonight.

It was her only chance at staying alive.

~

WHATEVER OIL THAT JUNE AND WREN HAD RUBBED INTO Tara had long since been sweated out. Aaloka hadn't gone easy on her. Tara's lower back hurt from having to stand so long. Her eyes burned even in the dim light. Her mouth felt dry, and she would have loved a sip of water between recitations.

But Aaloka kept barking out the names of herbs and medicinal plants, and Tara continued to recite her learnings back. Mistletoe. *Artemisia vulgaris*. Cow parsnips. *Monarda didyma*.

Tara refused to give up, or give in, or sit before the other woman did. She knew this material. She was damned if she would fail this part of the test.

Finally, Aaloka picked up her book one final time and nodded at Tara over the edge of it, giving her a big smile. "You did it!" she said. "Congratulations!"

Tara paused, waiting for the next plant to be named. "I did?" she asked. Now, she felt stupid, her head drained of all the knowledge that she'd crammed in.

"You did!" Aaloka said proudly. She leaned closer to Tara and said spoke in a very soft voice, quiet enough that those standing beyond the glass outside couldn't hear. "Not everyone in the coven felt that you could pass this part. I had to give you the toughest test, covering almost all the material. But you proved that you're a worthy candidate for the circle of breath."

Tara nodded, the relief making her sway where she stood. Kyle hadn't said anything about such a long verbal exam. Then again, he hadn't had parts of his coven actively working against him.

Could Tara continue in this coven? If she passed into the circle of breath? She couldn't go back and join Miss Lucy's. Would any of the covens in Portland take her? Or would she always be considered bad luck?

Tara bowed in return to her teacher, and then turned and bowed to the silent observers just outside the window. She used her tiredness to keep her pride at bay, keeping her smile and her stance humble.

In some ways, the oral test would be the easiest part for Tara. She had an organized mind. Despite what Aaloka said about Tara getting in her own way, she knew that she'd passed this part through strict discipline. (And a lot of cramming.)

However, to be a truly powerful witch, you needed not only discipline but imagination. Tara had never once been accused of being too imaginative, not even as a child. Even when she'd started coming into her powers, she'd spent very little time believing that she was imagining things and instead starting to test out what her limits were.

Miss Lucy had said at the time that it was a sign that Tara was destined to become a powerful witch, since she'd been so accepting of her powers.

Tara could only pray that Miss Lucy was right, as all of Tara's powers were about to be put to the test.

THE NIGHT HAD TURNED COOL, CAUSING GOOSEBUMPS down the back of Tara's neck. Even with the city lights, Tara could see a few stars peeking out at her, encouraging her. No breezes lifted her hair and the smell of roses and jasmine lay heavy in the air.

The coven of witches formed a circle on the first tier of the backyard, twenty one of them that evening. Sheila stood in the middle, leading the prayer, celebrating the journey of the light, reminding them that light flowed into darkness then back into light, the continuous cycle of life, death, and rebirth.

Tara tried to pay attention, to be present in the moment, to focus on welcoming the light, how good it felt to stand with her sisters and brothers in prayer, sending blessings out into the world.

However, her mind couldn't help but flit away, thinking about her upcoming ordeal. She was certain that Sheila would "cheat" and throw things at her that weren't normal or necessary for someone at her level to overcome. She'd asked Kyle about what to expect, but there hadn't been enough time for him to truly prepare her.

She should have reached out for help earlier. She had a network of friends who would have done what they could. Instead, she'd relied too much on herself and not on her community.

If she was ever in this sort of situation again, Tara vowed to reach out for help and support sooner. And to keep her reach broad as well, as Richard had been the one who'd come up with some of the more useful information Tara needed.

She finally wrangled her thoughts back into the here and now when Sheila started talking about the sister passing within, how Tara had to face passing from the internal world of thought to the external yet still internal world of breath.

"Blessed be," chanted the rest of the coven as they let go of one another's hands, stepping back.

"Come face me," Sheila intoned, beckoning Tara to walk forward.

Wren appeared at Tara's side, tugging on her sleeve.

Tara nodded and quickly stripped off the external cover. The air had grown cooler, but Tara didn't allow herself the privilege of feeling it. Instead, she stood tall and proud before the head of her coven. Tara called on her power, to strengthen her and give her grace. Her blood warmed, setting her skin tingling. The night grew brighter and her sight, clearer.

Sheila kept her face neutral, though Tara could tell the other woman didn't approve of something.

But Tara had nothing to be ashamed of, either the desire to advance herself or her completely naked state.

"To pass from the circle of thought to the circle of breath, you must walk the entire meditation maze unaided," Sheila said. "Save for your own powers and the blessings of Brigid and Samil."

"I am ready," Tara said, nodding her head once.

"If you fail to enter into the heart of the maze and reach the gazing pond in the center, you may try again in six months, during the winter solstice," Sheila continued.

There was a falseness to Sheila's words. She obviously didn't expect Tara to pass, but also, that she assumed that Tara wouldn't be around in six months.

Did any of the others hear if? Tara wouldn't break her gaze with Sheila in order to check. But she heard a shifting, as if some of the witches just shuffled their feet, uneasy.

"I understand," Tara said. "Thank you for the opportunity," she added.

Could the others also hear the unspoken *bitch* at the end of her statement?

No matter the outcome tonight, Tara was certain of one thing. She could no longer stay in this coven that had been the home of her heart for so long.

TARA STOOD AT THE START OF THE MEDITATION MAZE with her head bowed. It had been so much easier to defy Sheila with words and feelings. Tara had truly believed that she'd be able to walk the maze clear through to the center.

It was a completely different thing to be standing there at the entrance, faced with a cold, shifting fog that hid the stones just one step beyond. Weird noises came from the maze, sounding like the moans of the dead mingled with the whimpers of a wounded beast. They sent shivers down Tara's spine and cascades of goosebumps all across her shoulders.

She clenched her hands into fists, then opened them.

She could do this.

She took a deep breath of the clear night air outside the maze, ignoring the scent of rotten cabbage that blew toward her. Her power swelled, vibrating just under her skin like a second rapid heartbeat. She flexed her toes, feeling the solid cool earth beneath her.

After bowing her head in prayer for another long moment, Tara stepped into the maze.

The fog reluctantly crept away in front of her, like a cat slinking away from a larger predator. Tara felt the strength of the magic she faced, as prickly as blackberry bramble and as tough as old leather.

She kept her thoughts sharp as a knife, cutting through the tangle in front of her before she took more steps. Though she understood that it was better to walk straight through the maze, Tara was determined to take her time.

Most practitioners didn't have to face off against the head of their coven when passing into merely the second circle. That sort of strength wasn't generally called for until the final circle.

The next few steps felt lighter. Tara actually reached the first curve before the next attack came. It was subtle at first. She felt herself suddenly start to question her right to be there, to doubt her own abilities. For the first time, the thought came unbidden that she'd only made it this far through sheer luck.

Who did she think she was, believing that she could proceed?

Before she reached the end of the curve, Tara recognized the thoughts were not her own. She'd actually faced similar doubts when she'd walked the maze the first time.

Tara had studied hard enough, and knew the reality of her abilities, to banish the doubts. She had every right to be there, same as any of the witches standing nearby. She had power, she had lore, and she was learning the wisdom to know when to apply the others.

By the time Tara made it around the corner, the doubts had vanished. She could do this, though she recognized that if she hadn't been prepared, those thoughts might have derailed her.

The next few steps brought fear. Icy cold fingers walked down Tara's spine, reminding her that she was naked, not even the slight barrier of clothes to protect her. She felt her breath suddenly coming in gulps, as if the air was no longer thick enough to support her. Her stomach felt knotted, the muscles drawn in tight. Her hands shook.

Tara stopped and shook her head. This fear wasn't real. What was she afraid of?

She snorted when she realized that whoever had started off with this spell had chosen the wrong fear.

Fear of failure? Come on. If she failed, she died.

The realization broke the spell almost instantly. Tara walked forward with confidence, reaching the far curve easily and starting to turn back toward the start.

She couldn't help but feel a sense of triumph when

she passed the entrance of the maze. She'd made it through the first circle. From here on, all the spells through against her were going to be from the second circle. No longer internal or thought, but external and breath.

Or wind.

The first breeze tickled Tara's hair, laying heavily against the back of her neck. Then it tugged harder. Tara tried to keep going, but it felt as though an invisible hand had grabbed ahold of her hair and wouldn't let go. Her head jerked back with her next step.

Ouch.

Was the wind tangled in her hair? Tara couldn't turn to look and see. Or had the wind just grabbed a fistful of it?

Tara panicked for a moment. What spell should she use? Did she know a spell? She faltered, her thoughts racing madly.

Then she made herself stop and take a deep breath, willing the knowledge to rise up from inside of her.

Ah. That one.

Tara quickly called up a smoothing spell, one that would uncurl leaves and straighten vines. She held the scents of the three herbs she would use to perform such a spell, lemon balm, rosemary, and catnip.

The wind let go. Tara had the strangest sensation that the wind had formed a hand to hold onto her hair, then, as the hand let go, it combed her hair through its fingers, a soothing feeling.

Perhaps that spell had been cast by someone who liked her, and who wanted her to succeed.

She wouldn't always be so lucky, though.

Tara made her way through the next few winds easily enough, either deflecting them when they tried to push against her and blow her off course, or by pushing them upward so she could merely bend over and pass below.

As Tara rounded the corner and was about to pass by the start of the maze again, she suddenly felt herself out of breath. It was as if all the air had been sucked out of the area. She strengthened her own breathing, but that just made her pant harder. Her vision started to grow cloudy as she gasped.

How did she make her own air? She realized this might be the most important spell for her to remember that night, particularly if she didn't succeed and the Riprap man came after her.

The answer came from the tears that squeezed out of her eyes. Water had air molecules in it. While the air itself might be thin, there was still water in it.

Remembering the purple heather, Tara brought forth the rain. Not a lot—just a light mist blessing her skin.

From the water, Tara drew the air she needed, and took the next steps forward, into her third circle around the maze.

Hot winds caressed her cheeks. The third circle was the heart, feelings, and fire. Fear gripped Tara again, but this time, it was the fear of the unknown. Black smoke rose up in front of her, hiding the untamed blaze in front of her.

This wasn't fair. She was only a witch of the first level, trying for the second circle. Not the third.

But Tara had known that this wouldn't be easy. She forged ahead. These were just illusions. Nothing that would permanently damage her.

Right?

The black smoke cleared and Tara faced the heart of the flames. There was no way to walk around it or even leap over it: the fire raged at least ten feet on a side, and far above her head.

It was just an illusion, though the heat felt real. Her lungs started to complain again about the smoke and the lack of clean air.

Kyle had told her about this spell, as he'd had to pass by when he'd moved into the third circle. She couldn't banish the fire. It would drain her completely if she tried. She couldn't get around it either. She had to pass through it, using the right spells to protect herself.

Again, Tara called up the soft rains, just enough to drench her skin with moisture. Then she added tarragon to the concoction she was blending in her mind, and soaproot, to help her glide past. Then she added the last important herb, tansy, to make her invisible, so the flames wouldn't notice her passing.

Thus armed, Tara forced herself to step forward.

The intense heat nearly made her lose her footing, but she made herself take another step.

Then another.

Though Tara wanted to race through the flames as fast as she could, she knew that would be a mistake. The first would just chase her. Instead, she paused in the heart of the fire, marveling at the different colors, at how the flames whispered to her of ancient knowledge, how their nature was divided and their hidden god actually two-faced, one for destruction and the other for protection.

Tara felt blessed when she stepped beyond the fire, as if her pool of lore had just deepened significantly.

Whoever had devised that spell for her hadn't anticipated her not only facing the fire and stepping through it, but learning from it.

Tara didn't have the time to speculate on how this knowledge felt different. It was a well-accepted tenant that all lore was passed down from one witch to the next.

How much could Tara learn from the elements themselves?

Boosted with the confidence and the knowledge of the fire itself, she quickly passed through the rest of the tests of the third circle, ignoring the way her physical heart slowed as if it was threatening to go on strike and stop, as well as the building rage that came from outside of her, and the grief that struck her over her losses, both in the past as well as the present.

The next circle was stomach. Process. Water. Tara knew that she could pass through this circle easily enough. It was her element. She knew that she was more organized than others. Process was also her friend.

What Tara hadn't anticipated was the chaos of a raging river.

The banks weren't that far apart. Could she just step across?

No, that was a trap. She could tell by how wavy the air was on the far side. If she tried to leap or across, she'd land outside the circle. If she didn't carefully stay within the stone markers of each circle of the meditation maze, she'd instantly fail the test.

Could she walk through the water? Pass through it as she had the fire?

Except these waters were never the same. They were less stable than the flames. Each drop was separate, and it would be nearly impossible to bind them together to let her pass.

Tara snorted at herself when she considered the aspect of a bridge. That would help her pass from one bank to the other. But the waters wouldn't allow it, she suspected. She would get halfway across and they'd swamp the bridge deck, sweeping her away.

No, she had to stop the flow. Part the waters, like Moses had parted the Red Sea.

Tara started building a potion up in her mind. First, she'd need sandalwood and geranium oils to soothe the waters. Then she added a touch of ginseng to waken the senses. The sound of the water was too hypnotic for her. She was grateful for that knowledge, another thing to arm herself with.

For a moment more, Tara paused. Then she figured, why not?

Taking a deep calming breath, Tara called up the flames she'd met earlier.

Was that a gasp she'd heard from her unseen audience? Tara wasn't certain.

The flames came easily to her outstretched hands. She directed them down, toward the water. It parted easily, its mortal enemy driving it back.

Tara soothed the fires in her hands, sending out joy and playful thoughts. Fire was a dancer, pure and simple. The flames leapt forward, hissing at the water and sparking up with the winds. Tara welcomed the smell of smoke and the warmth.

As she stepped into the river bank, the mud oozed between her toes, cool against the warmth of her fire-heated skin. The smell of good earth rose up, comforting Tara. She could smell the herbs in the garden suddenly, the fresh rosemary, the spicy borage, even the sweet strawberries hidden in the corner.

Tara recognized the trap after just another step. The earth and its scents, brought to her on the singing waters, were there to distract her.

The fire in her hands would either leap away, unhappy at being contained, or turn around to burn through their container. The waters, in the meanwhile, would angrily swamp her as soon as she looked away.

Tara focused her thoughts back to the present, to pushing forward. The flames grew resentful at the continued fight with the water, spitting out sparks that burned the backs of her hands. The water, too, surged forward, angry at her chosen tactic.

Instead of taking her time passing through the river bank, as she had when she'd walked through the flames, Tara started to hurry, taking small, quick steps.

At the far edge, as Tara lifted one foot off the riverbed and onto the dry ground, the waters came surging back.

Tara recognized her mistake immediately. She should have backed out of the water. She tightened all the muscles in her legs, holding herself still, one leg in the water, the other on solid ground, not letting herself be bowled over.

First, she released the flames. She thanked them for their help, whispering the name of their hidden, protector god. Then, after taking another deep breath, she slowly pulled her leg out of the waters.

The river didn't have hold of her like the wind had earlier. Still, for all its rushing, it felt as though the waters were made out of solid, thick mud. Cold and clammy, and sucking at her, trying to pull her back down.

Tara got all but her foot free. The mud grabbed hold of her, tightening its grip. It was like sunbaked clay now, the smell of dry earth filling her senses.

No. This was all an illusion, though Tara still felt the stinging "kisses" the flames had left on the backs of her hands.

Tara tried to call up the wisdom from her studies, the spells she'd learned.

The thoughts that arose surprised her. Would it work? Or was it another trap?

Tara couldn't tell the difference. Her own powers were waning. She knew that she'd be a basket case for the next few days after this trial, her physical and mental strength exhausted.

Still, it was all that Tara could think of at this point.

She called the waters back.

The raging river answered her call. The loudness of the waters startled Tara, setting her heart to beating more quickly. The cold spiked through the bones of her leg, making her toes curls and her ankles ache.

But she didn't have to hold her awkward position for long, one foot on dry ground and the other stuck behind her. The waters did what she'd hoped they'd do.

They melted the mud holding her.

With a sucking popping noise, Tara freed her leg.

For a moment, she balanced on a single foot. She wavered from side to side, almost tipping over.

If someone had been cruel, at that very time, they could have sent the slightest wind against her and Tara would have fallen over, stepping outside of the carefully laid out stones.

Instead, after a few moments of a flailing half-moon yoga pose, Tara composed herself and brought her legs together, bringing her hands into prayer pose over her chest, her head bent and her eyes closed.

She thanked the goddess Bonana for the water, the hidden gods of the fire, the god of the earth and the goddess of the air.

She had made it through most of the circles, though. Learned and grown through levels one through four. She only had two left to pass through. She was so close to finishing.

Though her strength was low and her arms and legs were shaky, Tara raised her head defiantly and stepped forward again.

Bring it.

~

TARA WASN'T SURE WHAT THE NEXT CIRCLE, SEX, roots, or earth, would bring. Kyle hadn't yet passed through that circle. Her initiation to the inner circles had been nothing like his, however. He hadn't been tested as hard as she had been.

Was she stronger than she'd originally believed? Aaloka had hinted at that. Miss Lucy, as well. Tara had ignored them. She was just a late bloomer, and the magic came easier to her because she knew herself, better than a twenty year old did, that was for certain.

And so much about power and witchcraft came from knowledge, not just lore but of self as well.

Still, how many witches learned from the elements themselves? Listened to their quiet whispers?

Tara had often felt that the plants also spoke to her, telling her the best way to use them for a particular spell or oil. Sometimes the properties were similar to what she'd been taught. Sometimes, though, they were different.

Tara had resisted listening to the plants for their knowledge. It wasn't that she believed that she hadn't heard them. She knew that she had. But that lore was unknown., and she didn't know if she could trust it.

Now, she knew she could.

As she rounded the curve and stepped into the circle of roots, a loud cacophony of voices struck her. She shook her head, surprised. Where was that coming from? She stopped for a moment and looked around, trying to determine the source.

It finally occurred to her that she could now hear every single plant in the backyard. Each of them were calling her name, demanding her attention. They wanted to tell her all their secrets, sharing the gossip they'd heard from the bees, complain about their roots being cramped, how they needed more water, or less, or how their neighbors were crowding them.

This had to be an illusion. All these voices would drive Tara mad. The plants couldn't talk with her, not really.

She banished the voices, shutting off her special hearing, diminishing her power, bringing it back to just herself.

She took a step forward, then another, then had to pause again.

When the voices had vanished, the ground beneath her had died.

She could no longer listen to mother earth, herself.

Crap.

This was a test of balance. She had to find that fine line between too much power and not enough. Had to figure out how to allow herself to feel the world around her while at the same time, not be overwhelmed by it.

Grounding herself didn't appear to help. That just dragged her feet under the ground, making her as immobile as a tree. She needed to be more like a vine, traipsing along.

But that didn't work either. The first, initial root took hold and held her in place, stretching her and her awareness out until she thinned so much she was afraid she'd snap in two.

How could she move forward, allowing some part of the voices in? How could she be grounded yet still moving forward? Plants put forth runners, dropped seeds, or blew in the wind. They didn't pick themselves up and move.

Tara felt stymied. Her anger at being tested with such difficult assignments came back. She felt herself flare in anger, the fire she'd befriended earlier heating her skin.

She knew that she didn't burst into flames, though she wanted to, in protest of her treatment.

Instead, she calmed the fire inside of her, banking it into a warm glow, adding some water and wind to it so she wasn't stuck there either, constantly angry and bickering.

Tara opened herself up to the voices again, holding onto her own core tightly. The plants couldn't overwhelm the fire burning at her center. The scent of the roses and cool grass washed over her, all the herbs in the garden taking their turn to greet her, turn her fingers green, wind across her toes and around her ankles before leaving again.

Finally, a single voice rose above the others. It was the old oak tree that provided shade across the bottom of the garden. He spoke slowly, but with authority. He had no use for those flashy maples who colored their leaves in the fall, then discarded them without a care. He held onto his old, brown leaves, proud of how they crinkled with age. He didn't release them until the spring, when his children would need the nutrients and grow.

Tara lumbered forward, heavy with the weight of the tree growing inside of her. She still had need for motion.

After a few dragging steps, she was able to pose her

question for the oak: did he move through his children? Was that the secret of this level?

The amusement of the oak came in the quiet rustling of his leaves. No. That was not how he moved along.

His children had only slight awareness. It would take years for them to grow into themselves.

No, the way he moved along was by finally dying. He would fall over in place, his long trunk shattering as it struck the ground, the core of him finally releasing as he died.

In the spring, all his children would have a touch more awareness and strength. They would carry forward, each and every one of them, passing what they could onto their children until they, too, died.

It was the circle of life. The ultimate passage that the oak had to teach Tara. How to live fully each spring, falling back in the winter, living, dying, and being reborn. That was the only way to move along this circle.

Tara stopped her halting progress. She wasn't like the oak. She couldn't die just to be reborn. She had no children to pass her awareness to. How could she move through this circle?

Yet, Tara knew that the oak was right. Sex and procreation were the ultimate form of immortality.

Tara let consciousness fall into the earth. This time, instead of halting her progress or deadening the voices of the plants above her, Tara felt and heard everything. Their roots tickled her back as she inched along, undulating her consciousness like an earthworm. She felt the world around her dying as winter storms struck, the cold frost sinking deep fingers into the earth, slowing her progress.

Tara felt herself die as the winter continued. All thought ceased. Her breathing slowed to nothing. Her heart stopped its relentless beating. The fire at her core dimmed as the waters rushed around her, the winter rains blessing her skin.

Warmth came from an unexpected source: the very earth itself. Tara felt herself cradled in the embrace of the ground, the very world singing to her, calming her fears, lulling her to sleep.

The core of her being never went completely out.

Then spring arrived.

Tara's consciousness rose back to the surface, inch by slow inch. The sun had returned. The rains felt warm, now, not the stinging ice of the fall and winter. Her body felt full of promise and the rest of the plants sang to her again.

Finally, Tara rose the full way back up. It didn't surprise her to see that she was almost at the end of the circle.

She'd followed the complete path, from living, death, and rebirth. That had moved her along the circle, her feet numbly following as she dreamed the big dreams, sang lullabies with the earth.

Humbled, Tara finished the cycle of roots. She was such a tiny part of such a bigger piece. She wordlessly thanked the oak for his wisdom, the fires that had kept her alive, and the earth herself.

Never had Tara felt so connected to where she stood. The present beat loudly in her ears. She knew that she had to progress beyond this moment, but she still stood for a few long moments, drinking in the world around her.

Bowing her head one last time, Tara stepped forward again. She only had a half-circle to complete, before the maze circled around to the center gazing pond. She was so close.

She no longer felt as defiant as she once had. Her teachers had tested her further than most, demanding more knowledge than she'd been taught. Anger still burned at her core over the unfairness. However, if she was to fight the Riprap man, she needed all the knowledge she'd gained over the course of the evening.

How long had it taken her to pass through the circles? When she let herself think about it, she felt completely drained, as if she didn't want to take a single step forward. Her hands had a tremor to them that she couldn't stop. Power now passed straight through her: she had none of her own to call on. Her heart labored, beating despite how she just wanted to stop.

Still, Tara took the next step, into the final circle. She'd come this far. Just a little ways longer, and she could make it. She could be recognized as a witch of the second circle, though she felt as though she'd passed through many circles that evening.

Tara looked around, seeking the next test. Where would the final threat come from? What sort of trial would the final circle entail?

Yet, Tara felt nothing. The night cleared. She saw her onlookers gathered in a line at the back of the second tier of the backyard. Some looked angry. Were they upset with her passing? Or at the severity of her tests?

She couldn't puzzle that out now. She just had to survive the last one.

Step after step, the path remained clear. Tara was almost to the final curve. She could see the dark gazing pond, brimming with clear water, at the center, just to her left. Just a few more steps…

Ropes appeared out of nowhere. Heavy, twisted sisal, the kind used on the big boats, as big around as her forearm.

These were the ropes that the Riprap man would use to bind her.

They slithered on the path in front of her, blocking her way. They made a rustling noise as they moved across the earth. The smell of the river washed over Tara, filling her with dread.

Where was this coming from? Had Sheila saved up the scariest illusion for last?

Or had Tara herself provided the illusion, manifesting her worst fear?

Tara stood rooted to the path for a moment too long, not seeing the trap until it was too late.

The ropes had gotten behind her. With a sudden strike, as painful and shocking as a cobra bite, a rope thwacked against the back of her right calf.

Tara couldn't help but take a stumbling step forward.

Directly off the path, stepping across the stones and into the previous circle.

A sigh went through the night, the wind blowing the sound of mourning past Tara.

She'd failed.

Regret clenched her stomach. Her mouth filled with sour bile. She'd come so close.

Then the burning rage rose up. It was unfair!

Tara raised her head and stared hard at Sheila, the head of the coven.

The old woman stared back hard at her.

She had no regrets.

Aaloka and Kyle strode over to where Sheila stood. Tara knew they were arguing with her, expressing their anger at how Tara had been tested. She couldn't hear the words, her own heartbeat pounding too loudly through her whole head, her temples throbbing.

Tara had passed through all the other circles. She knew that she could have made it through to the inner circle.

Sheila had cheated. The last test hadn't been merely an illusion. Sheila had physically manifested those enchanted ropes. There wasn't any way for Tara to have avoided them.

They still lay curled at her feet, the life having drained out of them now that they'd struck their target.

The smell of the river encased Tara again. She shivered in its cold embrace. Gulls mournfully cried. The rushing of the waters blocked out all other sounds. Icy fingers pulled at her hair, pinched her skin.

You are mine.

The wind carried the words to Tara. She bowed her head again. The sense of death filled her. Only this wasn't a peaceful passing, unlike the oak. No, this was a death full of anger and pain, that sought to tear her soul from her flesh.

After taking another deep breath, Tara looked up again, defiantly.

The Riprap man was coming for her.

She was going to fight him with every ounce of her being. She had no choice.

CHAPTER 6

The river holds an angry god. It isn't that he hates just the newcomers, no, he despises all the life around him. He will not be tamed with mere words or simple deeds. He demands a sacrifice. Something great enough to satisfy his appetite, at least for a little while. Unfortunately, the river won't accept my companion Robin, something that I didn't learn until much too late. However, Robin and I passed a coven of witches two days earlier, a heathen group who spoil the sweetness of everything just to further their own selfish desires. Robin and I had talked about kidnapping one of their kind as a sacrifice. I'd thought to save time by using Robin, but the river god dislikes the witches even more. Something about soothing him when he wanted to rage. So I will make a pact

with the river god: give him witches as sacrifice, and he will hold back his anger against the bridges of the great city of Portland.

Wilson Evermore, magician and creator of the pact, 1899

TARA WOKE FEELING BRUISED. EVERY LIMB ACHED. HER toes and fingers felt swollen—hell, were swollen, so much that she barely had any wrinkles across the backs of her joints.

There were very few other physical reminders of her great battle. Her hands didn't hold any scars from where the fire had kissed her. Her head didn't hurt from where the wind had grabbed it and tugged on it.

The only other reminder was a five inch in diameter bruise across the back of her right calf, where the rope had struck her.

Kyle had explained as he'd driven her home that Sheila had gone too far. The rope had been real. All of them could see that.

However, Sheila had also defended herself by claiming that Tara was bad luck.

Aaloka and a few of the others had stepped back after that, had stopped trying to defend Tara.

Tara didn't blame them. For the good of the coven, she was the one chosen to be sacrificed.

There had to be another way.

Groaning, Tara pushed herself up out of her comforting bed. She'd already called into work sick that day. She couldn't face the shop, or to waste her last day by working.

She had to prepare. How, and by doing what, she had no idea.

But she'd think of something. After she woke up.

It was already ten AM. It had taken Tara over an hour to pass through all the circles, much longer than most. Then again, she'd had harder trials.

Tara took a long, hot shower. She was damned if she was going to be frightened of the water. It was her natural element. She could tame it if she had to. She was not about to let some asshole take away that simple enjoyment.

Still, Tara wouldn't let her guard completely down, even as she stood under the pounding hot water, soaping up her skin and washing the last of the oil away from the previous evening. She kept her wits around her, not letting her mind wander away. The fire inside her matched the heat outside, warming her all the way through and soothing away at least some of her aches and pains.

After Tara finished her shower, she slipped on her ratty robe and padded out to the living room.

Then stopped, stifling her scream at the last moment.

"Kyle? What the hell are you doing here?" Tara asked the man calmly sitting on her couch, reading something on his phone. He'd changed clothes, and wore a faded T-shirt with a quote about killing all the lawyers being a good start. (Which was funny, as Kyle clerked in a law firm, having decided early on that he never planned on moving up and being a full lawyer.)

"Taking care of you for the day," Kyle said slowly, as if explaining something to someone who was really slow. Which, okay, maybe Tara was feeling like that a little this morning.

"Did we talk about this last night?" Tara said. She had to admit that her memories were slightly fuzzy.

"We did," Kyle said. "You said I shouldn't. I disagreed. You told me to leave. I didn't. You need someone here to look after you this morning. And through the rest of the day, and into the night, as well."

"Thank you," Tara said. Stupid tears welled up. She was just overly emotional because she was so tired. She pressed her palms against her eyes, pushing out the moisture. After sniffing a couple of time, Tara finally felt ready to ask, "Can I make you some tea?"

Kyle gave her a big grin. "I'd love some."

Tara made him one of her special combinations. She started with a base of the salal leaves that she'd dried that fall, as Kyle didn't do caffeine. (Weirdo.) The salal gave the drink a green-tea taste, light and bright, with a hint of citrus. She used fresh leaves from her hyssop plant on the balcony, as well as a cutting of spearmint. Then she added a few of the strawberry leaves to smooth it out.

Kyle shook his head after she'd finished his concoction. "You know that some of the members of the coven are now referring to you as a hedgewitch, right?"

Tara shook her head. "Not sure what that means."

"A hedgewitch is a witch who's naturally trained, who doesn't study the lore. She's a common witch, the kind you'd find in the back country with a huge garden, who folks pay in milk and eggs. The hedgewitches are quite looked down on, you know, by us city witches."

"Okay," Tara said. "But I do have some lore."

"You have much more than that. You're a powerful witch," Kyle said.

Tara had been thinking about that since the trial. "No, I'm not," she said firmly.

Kyle raised both his eyebrows at her, looking dubious.

"I'm really not," Tara insisted. She sighed, trying to put what she'd experienced into words, force her tired brain to work. "I didn't pass because I was so strong or so special. I passed because I was able to listen and learn from the elements around me."

"Hedgewitch," Kyle said.

"Exactly!" Tara replied. "Anyone could do what I've been able to do so far. They just have to listen."

Kyle nodded, but didn't reply. Not until they were both sitting out on the balcony, enjoying their tea. The day had already started to grow hotter. Both boat traffic and car traffic noises floated up to them. The hummingbird thrummed past the balcony a couple times before he finally settled in for a long drink.

"I don't think that just anyone could do what you're able to do," Kyle said. "Hear me out."

Tara nodded, listening.

"You see these plants?" Kyle asked, indicating the long row of pots in front of them.

"Yes," Tara said. Almost every witch she knew of grew plants. It was the basis of their magic, the herbs and concoctions that they put together.

"How well do you think your plants are growing? Compared, say, to Patricia or someone like that?" Kyle said.

Tara snorted. "Not a fair comparison. Patricia has people for doing that sort of gardening."

"Exactly," Kyle said. "Kind of my point. But even, Han Su. Or me."

"You can all grow stuff," Tara said.

"But not in abundance. Not like you do," Kyle insisted.

"It isn't that I do that much," Tara pointed out.

"I believe you believe that," Kyle said. "And it might be that you don't do much. However, you care. You take the time. You listen and check in with your plants, trying to give them what they need. Am I right?"

"Yes," Tara said slowly. "They matter to me. I'd feel like a bad parent or something if I didn't try my best with them."

"Do they tell you what they need?" Kyle asked.

Tara rocked her head from one side to the other. "Not really. It isn't as if they talk to me."

Then she pressed her lips together, remembering all the voices of the plants the night before.

None of those voices had been foreign or strange to her. No, she was quite familiar with all of them. She'd just never really thought about it before.

Kyle just sat there, expectant.

"All right. Fine. Maybe the plants do talk to me. But it isn't because I'm special," Tara insisted, circling back to her earlier point. "They'll talk to anyone who will listen."

"And that's my point," Kyle said. "All witches, all of those people who have power, can hear. How many bother to listen? Then act on what they hear?"

Tara took a deep breath. She let Kyle's words settle into her skin. What Kyle was saying was true. "It was the only way I survived last night," Tara admitted. "Was by listening to what the fire had to say. And the plants. And the water."

"Exactly," Kyle said. "Hedgewitch. It isn't that you don't have lore. It's that you also have native lore, from the elements themselves."

"But how is that going to save me?" Tara asked bluntly. "I still don't know how to fight the Riprap man. And what will happen if I do get away from him? I don't want to bring bad luck to everyone else in the coven, even if they have turned their backs on me. Or even to Portland." Since this had started, Tara had looked up a couple of articles on the floods in Portland. While the area was less prone to floods than it once had been, given the sea wall and the other engineering feats that man had done to change the landscape, that didn't mean that it was impossible to flood the area.

Tara remembered a documentary on the floods in New Orleans, how it had ruined so many neighborhoods and lives. And the flooding that had been occurred all along the east coast.

No, there had to be a way to stop the Riprap man and prevent the next big flood from swamping the region.

Kyle stayed still in the morning air. "Would you say

that your greatest power is the ability to listen?" he asked after a bit.

"Possibly," Tara said. She'd never thought of it as her superpower before. But Kyle was probably right. She thought about how she listened to customers in the store and was able to match their needs, their true needs, with merchandise, no matter what words they used.

"So now we just have to figure out who you should listen to," Kyle said. "And how to give them what they want."

RICHARD CALLED TARA RIGHT AROUND NOON. SHE'D been planning on calling him later that afternoon if she hadn't of heard from him.

Tara and Kyle still sat out on the balcony, though Tara had changed out of her ratty bathrobe and into jeans and one of her favorite T-shirts, a pretty tie-dyed shirt covered in a random pattern of pink and blue splotches. Kyle was drinking a glass of homemade lemonade with a twist of mint in it, while Tara was on her second cup of black tea. Her brain still felt slightly fuzzy from the ordeal the night before.

"Hi, Richard!" Tara said brightly. "Got any good news for me?"

Richard gave a puzzled, "Hrmm? You were asking me to find out about the death of a relative."

"Yeah. What can you tell me?" Tara asked. "I don't really know much about Dorothy Parkerson's death."

Now Kyle gave Tara a puzzled look. She knew

she'd told him about visiting the witch guarding the Morrison Bridge. Had she forgotten to tell him about Richard looking into it?

She put the phone onto speaker and set it on the table, so that Kyle could hear what Richard had to say first hand and Tara wouldn't have to repeat it.

"It turns out that your relative was a small-time actress, here in Portland," Richard said. "So it was actually pretty easy to find information about her. Her death was officially declared a suicide, but there were a lot of questions about it."

"Like what?" Tara asked.

Kyle nodded, as if he was finally remembering what she'd told him the day before.

"According to the articles I read, rumors were that she'd just gotten a call from Hollywood. If she was just about to make the big time, why would she kill herself?" Richard said. "That was one of the big questions. But there were others."

"Okay," Tara said. "Tell me."

"Dorothy committed suicide by jumping off the Morrison Bridge," Richard said.

Tara couldn't contain her gasp. Luckily, Richard didn't hear it and just continued on.

"But the people who'd seen her that day all commented on how out of it she seemed. As if she'd drunk an entire case of bourbon, at least according to one of the eye witnesses. Her eyes were described as 'lifeless' before she climbed over the bridge wall," Richard continued.

"So was she drugged?" Tara asked.

"They didn't perform an autopsy," Richard said. "It wasn't required in those days. People knew she'd jumped off a bridge. There was some outcry after that as well, as people kept saying that there were fishy circumstances around her death. But the case was considered closed."

"That's really helpful," Tara told Richard. "Thank you."

"And there's something else," Richard said. "Now, I know you didn't ask for this. However, reading about this case reminded me of something else I'd read. In 1966, the Marquam bridge was completed. The day before the dedication ceremony, another woman committed suicide by jumping off of that bridge."

Chills walked across Tara's shoulders, sending cascades of goosebumps down her back. Her throat went abruptly dry. She took a swig of suddenly bitter tea before she answered. "That's really good to know," Tara said.

"If I go looking, I'll find a woman who committed suicide just about the time every bridge went under repair or was completed," Richard continued. "Won't I?"

"What do you mean?" Tara asked, caution overtaking her.

Damn it! That had always been part of her problem with Richard. The man was a completist. He always wanted to research every angle of something, willfully going down every rabbit hole he ran across.

"There are always women's deaths involved with the building or repair of every bridge," Richard said. "No one else has spotted the pattern, because it didn't always happen the day of the opening or dedication. Sometimes it's months apart. But there's always, *always*, the death of a woman by suicide as a bridge is being repaired or built when it crosses the Willamette River."

"I didn't know that," Tara said. Technically, she was speaking the truth. She knew that there would always be the death of a woman, but she hadn't known that they'd all commit suicide.

If that was even the case.

"You aren't feeling particularly suicidal, are you?" Richard asked bluntly. "Because the other thing that I didn't mention was that these always happened just after the solstice in the summer."

"Trust me," Tara said. "I am not about to kill myself. If I do die in the near future, no matter what it looks like, I didn't kill myself."

Kyle raised his eyebrows at her, but Tara stubbornly lifted her head, sticking out her chin at him. Richard was a dear friend and deserved to know.

"Okay," Richard said slowly. "What can I do to help?"

Tara smiled. "There isn't anything you can do," she said softly. "But thank you. Your friendship has always been important to me."

Richard sighed. "This has to do with the witchcraft, doesn't it?"

"What do you mean?" Tara asked, alarmed. She'd never told Richard that she was a witch. He was completely mundane. She couldn't tell him.

"I know you never told me about it, but I'm a

research librarian, and you left too many tantalizing clues over the years," Richard said honestly. "You don't have to admit it or to say anything about it. Just know that I'm here, and I support you, no matter what weird religion you may follow."

Tara rolled her eyes. "And how is being Catholic not a weird religion? I mean, come on, blood and body of Christ?" Though Richard was no longer practicing, he'd been raised Catholic.

"Hey! At least my religion doesn't support suicide," Richard said. "Does yours?"

Tara gave a great sigh. "No, it doesn't. Look, I have to go. But I will call you if I need any help, or anything looked up. Agreed?"

"All right," Richard said. "Look, your friendship is important to me as well. And I love you dearly. The world would be a much colder, and less weird place without you."

"And I hope that you can tell me that in person on Friday, when I get to meet your new girl," Tara said firmly.

"I hope that too," Richard said softly. "Goodbye, my friend."

"Love you too. Goodbye," Tara said all in a hurry before she swiped off the phone. Then she looked over at Kyle who was giving her the stink eye. "What?" she asked hotly. "I did *not* tell him anything."

"You left clues," Kyle said.

"I didn't mean to!" Tara replied. "He's just—he's like a dog with a bone. Won't give up. Which was why I stopped dating him years ago."

"But you're still friends," Kyle pointed out.

"I have a lot of friends!" Tara said. "Both inside the covens and outside of them." She was not about to comment on how few of her friends inside the coven had turned out to be true.

Kyle sat and thought for a while, contemplating his fingers tapping together. "Can he be trusted?" he finally asked. "If you did tell Richard the truth?"

Now it was Tara's turn to sit and think for a while.

"Maybe," she said finally slowly. "If I could convince him that it was really important, that the other witches might come after him if he knew and started talking about them."

Kyle nodded. "Then you may want to consider telling him at some point. *After* tomorrow."

"What? Why?" Tara asked, completely confused. Kyle was one who always stuck to the rules. It was one of the reasons why they always got along so well.

"Because you can't stay with Sheila's coven," Kyle said softly. "And I doubt there's another one that will take you. You're going to need to start your own."

All the blood left Tara's head, leaving her feeling dizzy. "I can't bring mundanes into a coven circle!" Such a thing was completely unheard of.

Kyle merely shrugged. "You're a hedgewitch. You can do whatever the fuck you want."

Kyle's statement, as much as the obscenity, struck Tara hard. He didn't normally swear. He'd used it for great effect, getting her to really listen.

"All right," Tara said after a moment. "I'll consider what you just said. *After* I survive the Riprap man."

Kyle gave her a bright smile. "You will. Now, let me tell you what else I've learned about Mulinohana, the river god."

Tara nodded, shoving her potential future aside for the moment. She could think about what it meant to be a hedgewitch, to be educated by the elements themselves instead of strictly through the lore of witchcraft, later.

First, she had another ordeal to survive.

TARA CALLED A MIDAFTERNOON BREAK, INSISTING THAT they leave the apartment and go walk around the block. She needed movement, not just studying. She longed to go for a long swim, though she doubted that was a good idea.

"So what do you think happened to the other witches who were sacrificed?" Tara asked Kyle as they started down the Riverwalk. A big tug was slowly making its way upriver, while a speedboat pulling a surfer made its way downriver. A nice breeze had started, cooling off the hotness of the day. The smell of the river turned Tara's stomach—she still remembered the feeling of the wet rope binding her wrists, how she struggled in her nightmare and couldn't get away.

"Now, you're saying that the souls of the witches lie underneath the bridges, right?" Kyle asked.

Tata nodded. "Trapped there by the Riprap man." She and Kyle had debated for a while about her going back to Miss Lucy to get another potion, so she could go and visit one of the other captured witches. She wasn't sure what they'd be able to tell her, though. They'd failed, and been captured. Maybe they could tell her what they'd done wrong, which could be useful.

However, what Tara really needed to know was what she could do right to avoid both the Riprap man and the potential floods all together.

"I'm wondering if the Riprap man took their souls the night before they died," Kyle said softly. "Their bodies had no choice but to leap off those bridges, trying to get back to souls, trying to make themselves whole again."

Tara nodded. The same thought had occurred to her. "So he tears the soul of a witch out from her still living body, then binds it. How does he do that?"

"You know that Miss Lucy would have a much better idea of how to go about that," Kyle pointed out.

"She was very clear about not wanting to see me again," Tara said. "I'm bad luck, remember?"

"Just had to ask," Kyle said, holding his hands up in surrender. "I'm not sure if knowing the exact process is as important as figuring out why he's doing it."

"It's to defend the bridges, right?" Tara said slowly. "The witch's soul acts as a guardian."

"Why?" Kyle asked. "Why would a witch go ahead and protect the place that she'd just been killed for?"

"Dorothy can't leave," Tara pointed out. "Cell sweet cell," she repeated.

"Imprisoning a witch's soul, and creating a guardian for a bridge, are two different things," Kyle stated plainly. "So which is it?"

"Hmmm," Tara said, pausing at the scenic view and

looking out over the water for a moment. The breeze lifted her hair off the back of her sweaty neck, carrying the scents of the water marshes just beyond the brambles at her feet. "Though it's a cell, as long as the bridge stands and stays strong, the witch will continue to live. So maybe she'll guard against it failing that way."

"That's possible," Kyle said. "But the bridge has to be under repair, or being built for the first time, for the witch's soul to be used. So I keep thinking that the Riprap man takes more than just their soul for the bridge."

"Wait a second," Tara said. She tried to remember something else that she'd heard. "Oh! I remember! It's the other version of London Bridges. It talks about taking a witch's heart."

She brought out her phone and brought up the children's song. She'd copied it down as closely as she could remember it after Davie had sung it to her. She showed it to Kyle.

Build it up with stone so strong,
Dance over the dead lady.
With a heart it will last so long
From a gray lady.

"So something about a witch's heart," Kyle murmured. "Heart. Feelings. Fire," he continued on.

"I think you're onto something," Tara said after a moment. She still felt the fire banked inside her, warming her core.

That fire was her heart. Somehow, the Riprap man wouldn't just take her soul, but her fire, her magic, her heart, and bind those to the bridge.

After another long moment, Tara finally turned to Kyle with a grin. "I think I have a plan."

CHAPTER 7

As a man of science, I can't help but question. How did the river god come to be? Was he always a god or at one point had he been a man? Without a doubt he is great and terrible. Like the angels, the first utterance he must speak for any coming into his presence is, 'Fear not.' So I have banished my fears and hold myself ready for his great plan. My thirst for knowledge is as boundless as the mighty waters in the river. I carry a part of the river god with me as I return to the shining city of Portland, along with the potions and spells necessary to bind a witch's heart to the next bridge, marking it as sacred to the river god, so that he will Know it and not damage it. I will mark all the bridges this way, as well as the city Herself, so that the devastation I saw at the beginning of my journey can never happen

again. This knowledge has changed me, but I'm willing to sacrifice myself to the greater good. I pray to all the gods that my success will inspire others to the same task; to denounce all witches, to be reborn in the fires of knowledge, and to purify themselves in the sweet waters of redemption.

Wilson Evermore, pact holder and witch hunter, 1899

TARA MANAGED TO SLEEP FOR A FEW HOURS THAT evening, in part due to the potion that Kyle made for her. While her body quickly succumbed to the soothing drink with peppermint, chamomile, lavender and red cedar, her mind continued to race with thoughts and plans. She dreamed of endlessly running away, the unseen monster behind her never quite catching her, but she never fully escaped either.

The dream faded after Tara awoke with her alarm, around ten PM. She showered again, then used the stimulating oil that Kyle had spent the afternoon making for her, rubbing it into every inch of her flesh. It smelled of pungent pine, ginger, new spring grass and wild roses.

Tara dressed in her ratty robe when she left her bedroom, walking into the living room. Sharon was already locked away in her bedroom, supposedly working on the next great American novel. Kyle had prepared as well. He looked like an oiled guard, his black skin glistening. He wore a brightly colored gold-

and-green striped vest, with no shirt, and loose brown-cotton pants that were cropped around the knees.

"Are you ready?" Kyle asked solemnly.

Tara shook her head no, but still replied, "As ready as I'll ever be."

"We have a little over an hour until midnight," Kyle said. "What do you want to do until then?"

Tara took a deep breath then let it out in a loud sigh. She honestly didn't know. What did you do the last hour of your life? She had no one to contact or hold. She had already done her best to prepare. Studying or learning anything more would just confuse her.

"What does your heart desire?" Kyle asked when Tara still hadn't answered.

Tara closed her eyes and *listened*.

"I want to walk next to the river," she said, surprised at the answer. She'd been avoiding the river walk for a few days, since this had all started. But she missed it. The river, for all its threat and danger, still held her heart in many ways.

"Then let's go walk," Kyle said. He lifted a single eyebrow at Tara when she walked to the door still only wearing her ratty bathroom.

"Look, we both know he's going after my magic as well as my soul," she said. "I may as well be comfortable defending myself."

"What, you think you're going to strip nude and distract him?"

"I have nothing to be ashamed of," Tara said. "And I don't think he's quite human. Besides, the strongest magic is generally performed without clothes on. You know that."

"I know that's what we've been taught," Kyle pointed out. "I've spent much of the afternoon questioning that learning."

"I understand," Tara said. "I've been doing the same. But this feels right."

Kyle gave her a sudden grin, the light of it warming her. "Then I'll make sure I have bail money ready if you get arrested for indecent exposure."

"What, you're not joining me nude to go dancing in the moonlight?" Tara teased.

Kyle gave an exaggerated shudder. "Gonna leave the dancing up to you, tonight, darling."

"Then let's go," Tara said. She turned and looked over her apartment for one last moment. She didn't know if this was the last time she'd ever see it or not. The living room didn't contain that much that was hers —the beige couch and matching loveseat had been Sharon's, only one of the standing bookcases contained Tara's books, and the small round table and four chairs were both Tara's and Sharon's, found used at a garage sale.

The balcony had all her plants, which she would miss. The kitchen was the heart of the place for Tara. She had an entire cupboard filled with her dried herbs and potions, oils and medicines. It was where she concocted her teas, which were as much a part of her magic as the spells themselves.

She was walking away from all of this, however. The material possessions had come to mean so much less in the last few hours. She and Kyle had prepared a will for her that afternoon in order to deal with them. She couldn't leave notes for her family—how to explain to them that she'd died at the hand of a supernatural creature?

Kyle accepted her keys, phone, and wallet, sliding them into various pockets in his vest. He'd take care of everything if…if.

She had to survive.

The air outside had a brisk chill to it. Tara pulled her robe tighter, questioning her choice. But she stubbornly didn't turn back, and instead, led Kyle through the locked gate of the apartment complex directly onto the river walk.

Dark waters ran in the river tonight, swift and deep. It had been a really wet winter, and the waters were still running high, even though it was already June. Above the rush of the cars in the street beside them, the cicadas gave their cycling call. The night smelled clean, the wind pushing away the stench of the city.

Without thinking about it, Tara turned automatically toward the Burnside Bridge. She knew that the choice was probably being influenced by the events sure to happen later that night. However, she also wanted to see the bridge, feel its strength and its structure, touch the iron and the concrete, listen to the hum of the cars.

They walked slowly up the pedestrian stairs, supported by separate pillars, not really part of the bridge itself, something Tara hadn't known until she'd started researching the history of the bridge. Tall banks of construction lights illuminated the bridge deck, banishing the darkness that Tara felt gathering around her. The smell of tar overwhelmed all the other scents.

Construction crews had narrowed the traffic lanes, so there was merely a single for traffic going either way. Despite the late hour, too many cars still wanted to cross. Their impatience was evident from how they would race forward whenever they got the chance. Tara counted at least three times when there was almost an accident if not for the miracle of modern brakes.

Kyle walked beside Tara, a pillar of strength. She didn't know how she could have survived even that day without him. "Thank you," she told him again as they neared one of the two fancy operator booths on the side of the bridge.

"No reason to be thanking me," Kyle said. "I was just doing what anyone with a heart should do."

A little anger seeped out with his words. That afternoon, Tara had just had a taste of how angry Kyle was at the rest of the coven for abandoning her, how betrayed he'd felt. They were his home, his safe place. That they'd abandoned one of their own had made him furious.

Tara's attention was drawn to the circle of silence that radiated out from the center of the bridge.

The Riprap man stood there.

He appeared mostly human, not made of riprap, as he'd appeared in her dream. He still wore an old fashioned suit, though this one was more formal, made of black wool and cut differently, with smaller lapels and a longer tail. Instead of a bowler he wore a top hat, also made of black, with a shimmering white rose tucked in along the brim.

She still couldn't see his face clearly. Instead, it appeared as though he had two dark ponds where his eyes should have been, and a gaping hole for a mouth.

Tara stopped. Kyle looked over at her.

"Do you see him?" Tara asked, not pointing directly at the Riprap man but waving in his direction.

Kyle looked forward, searching. Then he shook his head. "I sense a dark spot up ahead. Something I would walk around and say a blessing as I passed. I don't see a man."

"Okay," Tara said. She was a bit disappointed. She'd hoped that someone else would have at least been able to see what she saw. At least Kyle knew to avoid the spot where the Riprap man stood.

Tara turned to Kyle and held out her hands. "You need to stay here," she told him gently. "I have everything I need."

Kyle's hands wrapped around hers. She hadn't thought she was cold, not until she felt the heat of his palms against her finger. However, Kyle had a stubborn look around his jaw. "I still don't like this."

"I won't risk you," Tara said. "You've been such a good friend to me. I won't stupidly endanger you."

Kyle gave her a crooked smile. "Too late," he said.

Tara shivered as a searing cold wind suddenly washed over her.

The Riprap man stood beside them.

"Say goodbye to your lover," he instructed.

Tara stood her ground. "He's just a friend. And one of the best."

The Riprap man seemed puzzled. Tara could tell his attention had switched to Kyle for a moment. He appeared to be intently studying the man in front of him. Then the Riprap man shrugged. "No matter. I will take his life as well if you don't come with me."

Tara swallowed hard. This was it. Her fire and powers about to be tested, by a much crueler taskmaster than the head of her former coven.

The stakes were higher as well.

Tara let go of Kyle's hands, her fingers suddenly cold. But before she could turn completely away, Kyle suddenly wrapped his arms around her and engulfed her in an awkward, sideways hug.

"You can do this," he said gruffly, kissing the side of her hair. "I won't lose my best friend to this Goodwill hobo."

Tara nearly snorted out loud when she saw how the Riprap man stiffened at the insult, his anger apparent.

Was it because he was an ancient white man, still used to thinking of African Americans as barely human? It didn't matter. His opinion held no importance.

"I will survive this," Tara promised.

She had no idea if she could keep that promise, but she intended to fight with everything she had—lore, training, and talent—in order to survive the ordeal.

"You better," Kyle said as he let her go.

Tara stepped forward in front of the Riprap man. *Do your worst.*

The Riprap man nodded as if he'd heard her

unspoken challenge. "Witch," he said out loud, as if it were a curse word. "You are chosen."

A great sucking whirlpool of freezing water opened up at Tara's feet, sucking her down into the depths.

⁓

TARA FOUND HERSELF AT THE BASE OF ONE OF THE Burnside Bridge piers again, standing on the riprap. This time, heavy ropes wrapped not just around her wrists, but tied her body to the pier itself.

Dark waters surrounded her, billowing like storm clouds. The water tasted metallic, like cold steel. Cold pressed in on Tara from all sides, making her shiver.

She looked down, and found that her ratty robe had disappeared. For a moment, she was distracted and hoped that the robe hadn't been ruined. That was her favorite robe.

The ropes wrapped around her belly, then were looped around her shoulders, leaving her upper chest clear. Her legs, too, were tied tightly to the pier. She twisted, testing the limits of the ropes, but they didn't allow much movement.

Tara knew better than to believe that the Riprap man had left her chest bare so he could look at her tits, as nice as they were. He'd left that area clear so that he could rip the heart out of her body.

Surprisingly, Tara found that she could breathe easily underwater. Was that because her actual body wasn't down here? She hoped that Kyle was taking care of it, up on the surface, and would let it die if she didn't survive. She'd signed a "do not resuscitate" (DNR) order that afternoon along with her will.

She couldn't imagine how horrible it would be for her parents and friends if they came to visit her soulless body, kept alive by machines in a hospital.

The Riprap man suddenly appeared in front of Tara. She finally saw his true face, not the mask he'd worn before.

He was ancient. Furrows lined his forehead, then ran along the edges of his face, past his eyes and circling his cheeks, the skin sagging as if it were about to fall off. Age spots were splashed across his face, giving it a mottled look, as though he had a skin condition. His teeth had yellowed, and a few gaping holes showed through his ghastly smile. Watery, faded brown eyes covetously gazed at her. His suit hung loosely on his skeletal body. Bony hands formed into claws reached up toward her, as if to rake across her skin with his ivory-colored nails.

Everything felt as real as it had the night before, when she'd been tested in the meditation circle.

However, Tara knew that this was all, at some level, an illusion. Her body was still up on the Burnside Bridge, safe with Kyle.

The Riprap man started motioning with his hands, beginning an ancient chant. Tara could hear the words clearly this time, unlike in the dream. He was calling on the ancient spirit of the river, the god Mulinohana, to leave this bridge alone in exchange for the life the Riprap man was about to sacrifice.

Tara shook her head. The Riprap man thought he

was doing the right thing by sacrificing her, a witch. Didn't he realize that humans had already interfered with the course of the river? It was possible that the area could still flood, but that would mean a catastrophic failure all along the course of the river.

No, her death wasn't necessary to protect the bridges. Probably none of the modern deaths were.

The waters surrounding the Riprap man grew darker. Was that the spirit of the river taking shape?

Tara started her own prayer, not to the river god, but to the water, itself. She remembered its spirit from the night before, how strong it had run, how powerful it could be. It would not be beholden to anything as puny as a mere river god. No, water, the element itself, was who she called on.

The dark clouds billowing behind the Riprap man grew more solid. It looked as though a giant mass of seaweed was slowly forming, with a solid core body and hundreds of arms. It stank of rotting ropes and dead marsh lands.

Tara shuddered. It was a powerful creature, she could tell that.

Was this actually the god of the river? The spirit of the Willamette? Or some monster who'd usurped the title?

Tara used the prayer she'd used before to sharpen her thoughts, to bring the knife's blade of clarity to the bindings holding her. They felt as real as the rope that Sheila had used the night before, abrading her skin as she fought against them. They dragged her down as well, their weight preventing her from rising.

For a moment, Tara had a spark of hope, as her spell cut through a strand of the rope fiber.

She quickly realized that it would take too long. The ropes were as thick as her forearm. It would take forever to cut through it a strand at a time.

No, she needed something more powerful. She and Kyle had discussed the possibility, and had already prepared healing salves should she end up needing them.

Tara took a deep breath and prepared herself as best she could.

Then she called forth the fire banked deep inside of her.

Flames burst out all along the length of the rope holding her.

Tara screamed at the pain that engulfed her. The smell of burning flesh turned her stomach and made her wretch. But she wouldn't hold back, or recall the flames.

The dark mass in front of her drew back, as if afraid of the fire. The Riprap man continued his chant, speeding up when he realized his prize was getting away.

Tara hung in the pain as the ropes burned. Her thoughts grew hazy as she endured the agony. She struggled to breathe, as though the fire stole all the air from her. Even in the cold waters she realized she'd started to sweat, giving her own water to that surrounding her.

Suddenly, the ropes fell away from where they'd been wrapped around her shoulders and her arms. The release of the pain made Tara gasp. She lifted her arms, waving them in the cold water.

The pain around her legs slowed next. Tara kicked her legs to the side, the ropes dropping off like a dried mask.

The piece around Tara's belly burned on, but the pain had diminished to mere discomfort. When she looked down, she saw that a single piece of rope remained, wrapped firmly across her center.

Cautiously, Tara peeled the still burning rope from her skin. While the rest of body showed no trace of her recent agony, her belly had blisters on it, in a circular pattern.

Tara stood under her own power, facing the two creatures before her.

She was free. She knew that she could escape now. She had planted a strong rope herself, tying her soul to her body. If she reached out and twitched it with her magical senses, she could find her body. Possibly even rise out of this dream and flow back into it.

Plus, the bridge didn't really need her protection, not from a natural flood.

An unnatural flood, or these unnatural creatures in front of her, however…

The long arms of the river spirit slowly began to reach for Tara. She appreciated its caution. It knew that she could hurt it.

She'd proven herself a worthy opponent, even if she was a witch.

Now, she just had to turn the bad luck of the Riprap man away.

Tara bent her knees, bringing her arms up above her head as if she was about to dive into the water.

But instead, she dove head first into the embrace of the thing in front of her.

THE AMOUNT OF LIGHT SURROUNDING TARA SURPRISED her. She'd been expecting to be engulfed in darkness. Instead, a warm fire fed by rushes burned in front of her, brown flames cackling contentedly. The rest of the space around her was chilled, the air as crisp as a late fall morning. Mud squished between her toes. Her belly still ached. Though her physical body was somewhere else, she felt her heartbeat thrumming in the scars she now bore.

No words greeted her in this space. Instead, the water changed nature and tone, filling her ears with an amused chuckle at her audacity to seek the heart of it.

The Riprap man appeared beside her, still wearing his true face. The age didn't sit well on him. He had a sour look and a more sour smell, like an old man who'd spent his days eating cabbage. Close up, she could see his suit was actually tattered, the edges of the cuffs and collar ragged, the threads wearing thin.

"You don't need my soul to protect the bridge," Tara told the man. "The days of the massive floods are long over."

"You're wrong," the Riprap man said, shaking his head. "The river god demands a sacrifice. Something to mark the bridge as sacred. As his. Otherwise it will be taken."

Tara sighed. "The true spirit of the river would never demand such a thing," she said gently. "The waters themselves have no need."

Doubt crossed the Riprap man's face. Then he grew stubborn. "The river god has need."

"You're a fool," Tara told him.

"I've saved more lives than you ever will, witch," the Riprap man replied.

"Don't be too sure," Tara retorted, though she knew she didn't have a leg to stand on.

"If you don't believe in the river god," the Riprap man said, "then why have you come to the sacred hearth?"

"To bargain," Tara said honestly.

"The river god has no need for anything other than your magic and your life," the Riprap man sneered.

Tara didn't want to point out yet again that a true god wouldn't need such things. "Why mine?" she asked.

The Riprap man peered at her, as if she was an alien creature just born in front of him.

Surely the other witches had asked the same question…

"What makes me so special?" Tara insisted.

"Nothing," the Riprap man said firmly.

Tara felt the lie echo around the room. "That isn't true," she snarled. "Your river god wants you to tell me."

She felt it in the pressure of the water surrounding

her. The presence they stood before had a reason for choosing her. It wanted her to know.

The Riprap man shook his head, but still responded, "Because you do like the water," he admitted. "You're a witch, but you have an affinity for the depths. Not that it will save you," he added quickly.

"Did the other witches all have an affinity for the water?" Tara asked. Then she answered her own question. "No, they didn't. And this river god of yours is lonely."

The Riprap man blinked, surprised. "He has no other needs."

"None that he's told you," Tara said, suddenly feeling more certain of where she stood. "He wants more followers. He wants more believers. You've been a poor priest, as far as this river god is concerned."

"I've followed the true path, learned the knowledge of the inner circles," the Riprap man contended.

"So you're actually a witch," Tara countered. "If you know the way."

"No!" the Riprap man denied. "I am no witch. I merely had to study my prey so that I could capture them more easily."

Loneliness washed through the space, a great echoing sadness that hurt Tara's soul. She felt a knot form in her throat, a hard lump of grief that made it difficult to swallow.

"No one will pray to you," Tara warned the river spirit. "No one will treat you as a god. But I can guarantee that there will be those who will scatter rose petals across your waters at the equinoxes each year."

"What?" the Riprap man said, affronted. "Who are you to make bargains?"

Tara gave him a soft smile. "I am a witch, someone with powers and magic, who has an affinity with the water. And you have outlived your usefulness." The rest of the words tumbled from her lips, passing almost without her knowledge. "As your own mentor Robin did, before you."

The Riprap man gasped and took a step back as if Tara had actually struck him.

"The river god deserves a sacrifice," he said, recovering quickly. He lifted his hands in front of him, as if to actually grab her shoulders and start to shake her.

"How about you?" Tara asked, sidestepping. She reached for a rope of awareness that she'd planted deep in her soul. "Why doesn't your river god take your soul for a change?"

Darkness rushed into the space, filled with the sourness of the Riprap man. The fire died with a quiet *whoosh*.

"I will sing songs for you," Tara promised both creatures as she tugged harder on that lifeline. "To you."

The scaly hands of the Riprap man grabbed hold of Tara's bare arms. She twisted her entire body, trying to break the hold. She couldn't see anything in the inky blackness. All the air fled her surroundings. She was drowning in glacially cold waters. She kicked away, trying to free herself. But no matter how she moved, the hands found her, held her tightly, and had started to draw her back in.

Despite Sheila having cheated Tara of her proper status, Tara knew that she was worthy of being called an initiate of the second circle. She focused on the air in the water, breaking apart the molecules, bringing herself bubbles of air to breathe.

Tara tried to call up the fire again, but she was too deep in the water's territory for it to suffer its mortal enemy's presence.

While the fire warmed Tara's skin in the icy cold, it couldn't spring forth again.

So Tara reached for the old oak she'd talked with before. The one who'd found its way to move on through death.

She couldn't die here. Couldn't let go like that. Her death would be true, the Riprap man would take her heart and suck it into himself.

But the river spirit understood the passing of the seasons, better than humans. It would make the Riprap man release her.

Tara called the oak to herself, called up the winter soul, the dormant self who could weather any storm, the ice and cold, sleet and snow.

Then Tara reached for the ground that she knew had to be someplace below her. She knew where her body was, had a vague sense of the direction where it lay. The opposite way must be down.

So Tara pushed her roots *hard* into the earth. Down she delved, far under the pilings for the bridges, far past the lining for the river, down into the mantle of the earth itself.

She planted herself, and then refused to move. To bend. To be pulled or pushed or prodded.

Her breathing slowed as winter overcame her. Her blood pulsed with the slow beat of the seasons. Her body grew stronger than the manmade structure above her.

It took her a while to realize that the Riprap man no longer held her. He had moved on.

That was the true nature of water. To flow away, seeking the lowest possible point.

Tara shook herself awake, rising slowly out of her dream of earth and roots, of rocks and river silt.

A battle still to the side of her, the Riprap man and his former god.

She watched for a moment. They both employed massive amounts of ancient magic, grappling for souls with unfamiliar power. The battle wasn't between light and darkness, but dark and darker. If they'd been above water, in the air, she expected she'd see fireworks and bolts of pure energy passing between them. As it was, the water muted and slowed everything, turning her view wavy and indistinct.

Tara wanted to stay and see who was victorious, but her body was calling her.

Sweetly, Tara rose through the waters, like a kingfisher returning to the air, rising above her hunting grounds and back up into the clear blue sky.

Tara blinked. "Oooof," she said as she took a deep breath, filling her lungs with sweet air.

Light shone behind her, and Kyle sat beside her. It took her a few moments to place where she as: one of the river walk parks. The dew had fallen hard, but dawn was on its way. The sound of the early morning traffic soothed her.

Just in front of her feet, the river ran, dark and solid, like black silk flowing from a loom. Warblers hunted for bugs on the water, while the robins chased across the grass for worms.

Tara shivered, then gratefully wrapped her ratty robe more tightly across her chest. She turned to look at Kyle, who was studying her carefully.

"Hi," Tara said. She suddenly felt shy around him. She wasn't sure why. But she felt raw and reborn, and wasn't sure what to do.

"Hi," Kyle said. "You back?"

Tara nodded. She reached out her hand.

Kyle took it and squeezed it, as if understanding that she needed something more to ground her.

"I'm back," Tara said. She swallowed and felt her shoulders drop further, relaxing into her new self. "I'm back—to stay."

Later that morning, Tara sat out on her balcony, recovering and reassessing, well, everything.

Had the river god won? Or the Riprap man? As she

felt no threat that morning, she'd assumed that it must have been the river god.

She needed to find a new place to stay, or at the very least, a new flatmate. She needed to find a new coven, or form her own, as Kyle had suggested.

And she needed to come to grips with the changes that her ordeals had wrought in her.

Tara had always felt so old fashioned, as she was the only person her age who she knew who didn't have any tattoos. She had a few rings curled around the top of her right ear, with only three small holes in her left lobe. She'd tried piercing her eyebrow, but it had never felt right. Same with a nose ring.

But now, she didn't have a tattoo as much as she'd been branded. The mark on her stomach from where the fire had burned her had appeared on her physical body. She had a circle of raised flesh on her belly now, about the size of her outstretched hand, with four characters enclosed in it. They looked like ancient Chinese to her, with squiggly long lines, but a casual search on the internet hadn't turned up anything.

She suspected they represented the four elements, air, fire, water, earth.

Why had she been marked with these? What did they mean? She wasn't imagining them. She didn't have that good of an imagination.

In time, she was certain she'd learn their true meaning.

Not everything could be explained to the beginning initiate.

A humming bird thrummed across the balcony, circling once, before settling onto its perch to sip at the nectar in the feeder. Then it flew up to the iron post holding the feeder. It looked at Tara, its head cocked to one side, as if asking Tara what she was going to do next.

"I don't know," Tara said, taking a deep breath. "But I have time, now, to figure it out."

The hummingbird *tsked* at her as if it was about time Tara finally understood that, before flying away to its busy tasks, leaving Tara her day.

EPILOGUE

I drag myself onto the shore just as the night falls. The battle had been epic. I have survived. The bridges and the city of Portland herself are safe once more. But the cost…Ah, the cost. I find myself shaken to my core at the powers I have gathered. I had no idea how I had grown. I am no witch. Yet, I have absorbed much of the magic I have taken for my god. Former god. My holy quest has been forsaken. However, I still live. I will find a new quest, new deeds that need doing, tasks that would offend the gentle sensibilities of these modern people. That, as well as have my revenge on the one who so upended my world. That thrice-damned witch. Tara.

Wilson Evermore, the Riprap Man, 2018

ABOUT THE AUTHOR

Leah Cutter writes page-turning fiction in exotic locations, such as a magical New Orleans, the ancient Orient, Hungary, the Oregon coast, rural Kentucky, Seattle, Minneapolis, and many others.

She writes literary, fantasy, mystery, science fiction, and horror fiction. Her short fiction has been published in magazines like *Alfred Hitchcock's Mystery Magazine* and *Talebones*, anthologies like Fiction River, and on the web. Her long fiction has been published both by New York publishers as well as small presses.

Find Leah's books on Knotted Road Press at (www.KnottedRoadPress.com)

Follow her blog at www.LeahCutter.com.

Reviews

It's true. Reviews help me sell more books. If you've enjoyed this story, please consider leaving a review of it on your favorite site.

Come someplace new…

Are you a traveler? Do you enjoy exploring strange new worlds, new cultures, new people?

Journey into the various lands envisioned by Leah Cutter.

Sign up for my newsletter and I'll start you on your travels with a free copy of my book, *The Island Sampler*.

I will never spam you or use your email for nefarious purposes. You can also unsubscribe at any time.

http://www.LeahCutter.com/newsletter/

* 9 7 8 1 6 4 4 7 0 1 0 1 0 *